Runner in Red

Jessica —

Runner in Red

A Search for the First Woman to Run a Marathon in America

TOM MURPHY

Thank you for the support the cause!

TM

Encircle Publications, LLC
Farmington, Maine, U.S.A.

Runner in Red Copyright © 2017 Tom Murphy

Paperback ISBN 13: 978-1-948338-02-8
E-book ISBN 13: 978-1-948338-04-2

Library of Congress Control Number: 2017962453

Editor: Cynthia Brackett-Vincent and Devin McGuire
Book design: Eddie Vincent
Cover design: Beth MacKenney and Deirdre Wait
Cover images: © iStockphoto.com and Shutterstock.com

Published by: Encircle Publications, LLC
PO Box 187
Farmington, ME 04938

Visit: http://encirclepub.com

Printed in U.S.A.

Publisher's Cataloging-in-Publication data

Names: Murphy, Tom Aloysius, author.
Title: Runner in red : a search for the first woman to run a marathon in America / Tom Murphy.
Description: Farmington, ME: Encircle Publications, LLC, 2018.
Identifiers: ISBN 978-1-948338-02-8 (pbk.) | 978-1-948338-04-2 (ebook) | LCCN 2017962453
Subjects: LCSH Boston Marathon--History--Fiction. | Women runners--United States--Fiction. | Marathon races--Fiction | Semple, Jock, 1903-1988--Fiction. | Switzer, Kathrine--Fiction. | Mystery and detective stories. | BISAC FICTION / Sports | FICTION / Mystery & Detective / General
Classification: LCC PS3613.U7555 R86 2018 | DDC 813.6--dc23

DEDICATION

For Caitlin and Justin, my siblings and my dear friends, the late John J. Kelley (Young John) and Jock Semple, as well as Johnny and Jessie Kelley's three daughters, Julia, Kathleen and Eileen. And for stars in my Boston Marathon galaxy. The list is long, but so is a marathon: Jan Greaney Clark, Gloria Ratti, Roni Selig, Jack Fultz, Amby Burfoot, Jim Roy, Tom Derderian, Dave McGillivray, Kathrine Switzer, Christy Olsen, Rich Horgan, Kara Corridan, Peggy Peters Fox, Richard Johnson, Bobby Hodge, Billy and Charlie Rodgers, Susan Hurley, Joan Kenney, Nancy Fitzgerald, Barrie Brett, Mark Longo, Terry Monell, Tom Morante, Joe Salois, Fr. Isaac Keeley, Mike Dunford, Janine Wert, Jessica Joyce, Bob Casey, Randy Thomas, Julie Heyde, Joann Flaminio, Gina Caruso, Bobbi Gibb, Karen Warner, Pam Steenland, Mary Ann Penglase, Marty Brown, Bill Kelly, Patti Catalano Dillon, Jerry Ford, Johanne and Terry Connors, the teams at Tracksmith, Regis College, Boston College, and cancerGRACE.org, the Villanovans (Kieran, Bob and Bob,) my legion of Murphy/Rice cousins and in-laws and so many others who have offered me inspiration and a life-time of Boston "running" friendship.

Proceeds from this book will support the RUNNER IN RED campaign (in partnership with the Bonnie Addario Lung Cancer Foundation) to cure lung cancer (see runnerinred.com) and Kathrine Switzer's charity project 261 Fearless to empower women.

INTRODUCTION

All great stories begin with, "What if?"

I was an aspiring writer working as a teacher in Boston Public Schools in 1980 when Jock Semple, co-director of the Boston Marathon, asked me to write his life story.

I jumped at the chance, since I was a runner and Jock was a legend. In 1929, he ran his first Boston Marathon after emigrating from Scotland. Nine times in the 1930s and 40s he finished in the top ten. In the 1950s, he took over operations for America's most historic race and in 1967, he made himself "infamous" by chasing Kathrine Switzer down the road in the Boston Marathon at a time when women were not permitted to run. He was not against women, or as he put it, "I was simply protecting the rules."

Each day after school I would sit in Jock's cramped cinderblock cubicle in the old Boston Garden where he worked as a trainer and a physiotherapist. I would write furiously with my pad and pen (no iPads in those days) as Jock's "patients," as he called his portly businessmen clients, teased him about his irascible responses to "cheats," including decades of chasing interlopers who tried to get into the Boston Marathon without conforming to the rules.

Oh, the stories, which became a book I co-wrote with John J. Kelley, winner of the 1957 Boston Marathon, called *Just Call Me Jock*.

It was an on-the-cuff comment by one of Jock's patients that triggered my long-standing interest in a "what if" that has led to this story that follows.

The fellow on the rubdown table asked Jock if he would have chased the "Runner in Red" in 1951, and Jock responded with a throw-away line, "If she woulda been real, I would have protected the rules."

"If she woulda been real..." caught my attention and sent me to the Boston Public Library to research the "Runner in Red."

I learned that this legend really persisted. There has been a long-standing belief that a woman slipped into the 1951 Boston Marathon undetected and ran the race, which, if that could be proven, would make her the first woman to have run a marathon on American soil. "She wore red," as claimed by a group of Canadian runners who say they tried to bring the matter to the attention of Jock and other race officials, but to no avail, their story was never corroborated, and so today the "Runner in Red" remains a mystery and an urban legend.

It remains a "what if" mystery I have long wanted to explore in novel form drawing upon Jock and all the wonderful stories I "soaked up" along with the liniment fumes.

This fictional account, a period piece set in the 1990s to coincide with the 2000 Boston Marathon, the Millennial Marathon, is my attempt to solve the mystery of that historical "what if" in the context of a love story and family drama.

I hope you enjoy the "run" with me.
Tom Murphy

CHAPTER ONE

September 1999

My name is Colin Patrick. For twenty-nine years before this story opens in 1999, I had been chasing love, luck, and stability, but swinging wildly and missing big in my search for the good life when I spotted a copy of *Runners' World* on my boss, Bridget Maloney's, desk in the newsroom of Philadelphia's Channel 7.

The magazine was open to a story about the explosive growth in women's running since 1972 when after a series of confrontations between women and race officials the Boston Marathon relaxed its rules and permitted women to compete.

"Women's running?" I said to Bridget as she sat at her desk to read the story. "I didn't know you liked sports."

"The Boston Marathon is planning a celebration of women at the 2000 Boston Marathon next April as they usher in the new Millennium and Roman wants us out front on the women's angle," she said. Steve Roman owned the station, but other than the huge portrait of himself he insisted be hung in the lobby he was a distant figure to me. "When 20,000 competitors toe the line at Boston on April 17, 2000 to start a new century, a third will be women. That's our story, sweetie, how so many women run today, yet so few know the history of women's running."

"I didn't know you were a jock."

"I love news. Pack your camera gear. We have a press conference at City Hall. Then we'll go to the track at U Penn to get tape on women runners for a feature I want to do."

I had other things I wanted to discuss with Bridget, namely, images that had begun to nag me in the mirror in the morning: sputtering shopkeepers, bumbling accountants, stammering non-profit executive directors, all with sins to conceal, and me with my camera poised to beam them onto the nightly news as Bridget shoved a microphone under their chins.

"Do you ever wonder, Bridget, if this is the day we send a bugger down a deep dark hole they never come back from?" I said, alluding to the director of a Food Bank in South Philly who had dropped to his knees and begged us to go away that week.

"It may seem odd," she said, continuing to read, "but for the first sixty-nine years of the Boston Marathon, until Roberta Gibb ran in 1966 and Kathrine Switzer was chased by Jock Semple in 1967, there were no female participants in the race."

I reached for the magazine to get it away, but she slipped it into her handbag.

"Do you ever wonder, Bridget, if any of the guys whose lives we break like glass might be innocent?"

"Maybe you need a change of scenery," she said with a wink. "Take the van, baby. I'll meet you at City Hall. Brown starts her Council meetings at 11 am sharp. Don't be late."

Bridget Maloney was a stunner as well as a crack investigative reporter. Late 40s, blonde, she had killer legs. Though she was single (separated from her husband in Boston, according to scuttlebutt around the office), I had never seen her date. Stories abounded, however, about her ability to impale a macho guy with a single sidelong glance. As well, she possessed a keen intuition to match her physical gifts. Certainly, nobody doubted her talent. She had worked at Channel 7 for three years and owned enough hardware, Emmys and other awards, to fill an aisle at Home Depot.

She was my best friend as well as my boss since she had hired me six months earlier. I was in Philadelphia at the time only because that's as far as my money and the bus from Chicago would take me after I got canned in the Windy City following a confrontation with the news director.

I couldn't take my eyes off her the morning I stepped off the bus from Chicago and spotted her setting up for a remote on Market Street. Her Gucci skirt switched side to side as she walked sending a signal to the world: step aside, people, I own this ground I'm moving across.

"I was at Channel 10 in Chicago," I said as I strolled over to her, stumbling from the too-many beers I'd had on the bus. I don't know why I pulled my Red Sox rookie card out of my wallet—twisted and faded as it was. Maybe it was the intuition I had that beneath the impenetrable shield she wore as a cover to the world she was kind.

She studied the card a long moment, a good sign.

"You hirin' cameramen, lady? I'm a good cameraman."

"Go away. Before I call a cop," she said.

So much for kind!

Two days later, I was sleeping on a bench at the 30th Street train station, still in town, when she tapped my boot with her dove gray Ferragamo shoe.

"Need a wake-up call, sweetie?" That's what she called me, sweetie, as I sat slouched on the bench waiting for a train to Miami, since I hadn't tried the south yet.

"So what is it exactly you told Sam Edwards, the news director at Channel 10 in Chicago, that he should put up his butt?"

"You talked to the Prince of Darkness?"

"I'm a reporter. That seems your pattern, to burn your bridges."

"I have opinions."

"Sam says you're incorrigible."

"He means incorruptible. There are lines I won't cross."

"Still follow the Red Sox since your playing days ended?"

"How do you know so much about me?"

She handed my baseball card back to me, which I didn't realize she had kept. "I research my subjects. That's what I do in addition to breathing."

"I'm a subject now?"

"I saw you play. You banged a double off the Green Monster the day I was at Fenway. So you want a job? Talk to me."

"I need a job, but I don't talk about anything anymore that requires my emotional involvement."

"Oh, my, sweetie, you do need my support."

That night I slept in a hotel, my first real bed in weeks, compliments of Bridget, and two days later Channel 7 hired me as her cameraman.

"Why are you doing this for me?" I asked as I cornered her near the watercooler that first morning.

"When you interrupted me on Market Street, I liked your eyes."

"How could you see my eyes? I was half asleep."

"I saw the other half. I'm taking a chance that you can find your swing again. But don't blow this, sweetie, it's not like you have any bridges left to burn."

We became inseparable after that, like two birds slicing through the crystal air, wingtip to wingtip.

Little did I realize, however, that she had another reason for hiring me: she had a plan for me, one that was about to send my life into a spin again, bigger than my collapse with the Red Sox.

The next several months with her would put me in the middle of the biggest women's sports story of the year, a women's story in a sport I knew nothing about, but even if I had known all the details about the intrigue to come I would have been powerless to resist Bridget.

4

For if there is one thing true about me, it's this: put me in the company of a strong-willed woman in motion and I will fall under the gravity of her spell every time.

I was halfway to City Hall when the phone rang in the news van. It was Roman, Jr., the owner's son, and the station's lead assignment editor.

"Reroute to Franklin Park," he barked. "An item just came in about obesity in America."

"Oh, wow, Junior, stop the presses."

Junior (he hated it when I called him Junior) was a pasty-faced kid with an instinct for the jugular and a newly-minted MBA from Penn, courtesy of his daddy's dough. I knew he didn't like me, which had been my liability at the three other stations where I had been fired in nine years since an injury cut short my baseball career: I could not conceal my disdain for prissy boys who flaunted their silver spoons.

"I want you to capture recreational runners, rollerbladers, whatever, in contrast to obese examples."

"Examples, Junior? We talking human beings here?"

"I want your tape on my desk in an hour," he said, ignoring my tone, and click went the phone because he knew I would never push back so hard as to jeopardize my gig with Bridget.

I shot a close-up of a 300-pound man draining a 32-ounce Slurpee, along with a shot of a young couple in purple balloon pants wolfing Nachos, when suddenly my shoe crunched something soft on the path, a pink fanny pack, and I picked it up.

When I looked up I saw a trim blonde girl, mid-20s, the fanny

5

pack's owner. She was jogging in place in front of me, her blonde ponytail bouncing side to side off one shoulder then the other.

She wore a tight red halter, microfiber of some kind, and red shorts that hugged her perfectly sculpted hips. I glanced at her bare midriff, and her flat stomach, beaded with tiny crystals of sweat, then I heard her voice, clear, but with an edge.

"Can I have my pouch back, *please?*" but as I lifted my camera and pointed it at her, her tone became very sharp, "Hey, what are you *doing?*"

"I'm going to put you on the news tonight," I said, focusing my camera on the terror showing in her amazingly blue eyes. "I need footage of fit people."

"I don't want to be on the *news!*"

"Wait!" I called, but she turned and I watched her long trim legs carry her away, her blonde ponytail slapping shoulder to shoulder again as she sped off down the path.

"Hey! What about this?" I said as I held up her fanny pack, but as quickly as she had appeared she disappeared around a cluster of bushes at the entrance to the park.

When I opened the pouch I found no indication of her name, only three bucks, a gold medal with blue lettering, "Boston Athletic Association, 1951," and a number for a road race with big red lettering, "F-1."

F-1, she must be good, I thought as I returned to my van, followed by my next thought: *how does a guy get a chance with a girl like that?*

As soon as I got back in the truck, Junior came on the radio again.

"Media 17. Change your route again. I want you to go to City Line Ave. and the Pike."

"I told Bridget I'd meet her at City Hall for a Council meeting at 11."

"That meeting's been canceled. The City Council President got in a car wreck."

"How bad?" I didn't know the Council President, Priscilla Brown, but she was a Hillary Clinton type, feisty, good copy.

"Real bad. I'll have Bridget meet you at the scene."

It was bad. I saw that immediately as I approached the crash site where a cop waved my news van through the morass of traffic before directing me to a spot between an ambulance and a shattered vehicle, a Honda Civic.

This was Brown's car, obviously, and I craned my neck to catch activity inside the ambulance, but I couldn't see through the tinted windows. The Honda, on the other hand, looked like a crushed can. That along with the slow turn of the ambulance at the top of the block told the tale: Priscilla Brown, Philly's rising political star, could not have walked away.

"Colin?" Bridget shouted, as she rapped on my driver's side window. "Junior wants us to go to Haverford County Day School. He's got an angle for us."

The school, on the grounds of Haverford College, was about ten minutes away. "What's there?"

"Just drive," she said, as she hopped in on the passenger side. "We'll see when we get to the school. Hurry."

A guard waved us through the gate at Haverford as the van's squawk box reported the news on Priscilla Brown, that she was DOA at Pennsylvania Hospital. Bridget motioned to me to drive up a winding, tree-lined path, to a building where the sign read, "Day School."

"Park here," she said. "I'll call the station."

A bell rang inside the school and I removed my camera as a dozen small children, seven or eight years old, came running out to play for recess.

"What's our story?" I said to Bridget.

I could hear Junior as she got him on speaker: "Brown's kid goes to school there," he said. "Get him on tape for an exclusive before the other stations get there."

I grabbed the phone out of Bridget's hand. "Are you out of your fucking mind, asshole?!?"

"Give Bridget the pictures she needs for this story or you can pick up your money, son," he said loud enough for both of us to hear.

"I don't need your goddamn money," I shouted into the phone, and I set my camera on the ground.

"Colin," Bridget called, but I walked fast along the path to the gate. "Where you going?"

"Screw Junior and the horse that brought him," I shouted over my shoulder as I picked up speed heading to the gate, but she jogged after me and caught me quick.

"Three stations, right? And this will make four you burned bridges at."

"The boy lost his mother, for chrissakes, Bridget, and Junior wants us to put him on the six o'clock news."

She grabbed my arm. "Junior's a termite. Why throw your life away again?"

I felt my heart pounding. The only sound was the laughter of the children playing on the hill.

"Because I had this happen to me," I said looking her straight in the eye.

"What?" she said, and she let go of my arm. "What are you talking about? Happened to you? What happened to you?"

"Never mind," I said, but she chased me again and caught me at the front gate.

"Wait," she said, as she spun in front of me and blocked me with her slender frame. I could feel her breast against my arm and I could smell her perfume.

"I don't have a lot left, Bridget. But what I do have I want to hold onto."

She looked deep into my eyes, then she pulled out a pad of paper and scratched a name and a number. She tore the page from its sheath and pressed the paper into my palm.

"What's this?"

"A number."

"For what?"

"For a guy at a station in Boston."

"Boston?"

"Stan's the news director there, tell him he owes me one," she said, and she tapped my hand with the note. "I'm building you a new bridge, kid."

"I don't need your bridge."

"Oh yes, you do," she said, and she kissed her fingertips before pressing them to my cheek ever so gently, then she smiled.

"Trust me, sweetie."

CHAPTER TWO

t was an 0 and 2 count I recall vividly as I toed the infield clay at Fenway Park waiting for the pitch that night in September, 1990. A cold drizzle leaked from the charcoal sky as Roger Clemens, our pitcher, looked in for the sign and I tapped my glove thinking: *hit it here!*

I had passed up a scholarship to Notre Dame for the chance to sign with the Boston Red Sox in June after high school, but the bet looked like a smart one as I hit .356 in twenty-one games following my September call-up, and already the front office had dubbed me, at 19, their "shortstop of the future."

"This is the preview, the coming attraction," the general manager told the Boston Globe in 1990. "We put the kid in the middle of the action, but he plays like he's been up here his whole life."

How long ago since the fly ball that cut my career short with the Red Sox?

Ken Griffey, Jr. of the Seattle Mariners waved his bat, as I shaded him toward third base—an eon ago—expecting Griffey to slap the pitch.

But he popped it up.

I remember the arch of the ball as I scooted on the grass behind the bag at third, and I glanced away one second to gauge my distance from the spectators' rail. When I looked up again, searching the black sky illuminated by lights, I found the ball dropping fast and I raised my glove. But my ankle did not follow the pirouette with the rest of my body. Instead, my cleat locked under a brace that fastened the rail to the field, and a moment later I felt the crunch from my hip down, like a bat splintering, as I tumbled into the laps of scattering fans.

Torn ligaments, broken fibula, decimated ankle: the doctor's report testified that my leg looked like it had passed through a butcher's shop.

Nine years ago, almost ten. An eternity!

I played in Puerto Rico the next winter and the Red Sox gave me three seasons in the minors to find my quick bat again, but the soft tissue in my ankle never healed and that was it—my life had ended in foul territory in the rain in Boston at nineteen.

My mother had a favorite saying when I was growing up: "Everyone has a diamond inside them," she said. Though most people cake their diamonds with bitterness, pride, and regrets, their diamond is still there, shining at the center, waiting for them to discover it, she believed.

Challenging words, but the box score on my life was showing "E" for "Error."

I bounced around the country for six years after the Sox let me go, searching without success for a passion to replace my love for the game. I worked at a series of jobs, including stints as a television news cameraman, a trade I had learned from my dad who had been one of the best news shooters at NBC in New York.

"If you want to be an eagle, you've got to fly like one," my mom had always told me, so I kept going, pushing ahead, because I wanted to be an eagle.

She had great energy and a wonderful laugh. That's what I remember most about my mom, the way she would throw her blonde head back and laugh in response to the ladies who sat with her at my little league games when I was a boy. They would chide her for giving up Europe and Asia and other places she had trekked as a foreign correspondent for UPI to be a mother in Hicksville, New York, editing the community weekly.

"You don't understand," she would tell the ladies. "This is what I've chosen. Family is everything to me."

I was nine when she died. My father, who had survived a bullet in the Korean War, barely survived the loss, and I doubt I have yet.

I don't know why women's ambitions fascinate me more than men's, but they do. Male posturing, designed as it is to gain an advantage, has always bored me. But a woman with a mind of her own and the kick to back it up, I will surrender to every time. Maybe that's why as the days in Boston turned to weeks without producing traction, still I couldn't get Bridget Maloney out of my mind, and I wondered: *did I make the right choice leaving her?*

I found an apartment over a tavern in Revere, north of downtown, when I arrived in Boston. The place had 35-cent beers and a portrait of JFK on the top shelf. The room was cheap, which was good, but the ladies who came out at night in hairnets to shout their husbands off the barstools (and their husbands who resisted) got to me. I clung to a loftier view of relationships, so I found another place—this one over a tavern in Dorchester, south of downtown—where they let me tend bar for extra cash. The floors of the apartment tilted higher at one end than the other, same as the first apartment, but at least it was quiet at night.

The luxury came at a premium, however, so I had to take a second job with a temp agency, one of those Work-Today/Get-Paid-Today outfits, to make the higher rent. The temp manager, Friar Tuck with a nose ring, gave me the address of a storefront in the South End with instructions to create a mailing list for a celebration of women runners planned for the 2000 Boston Marathon next April.

"The clock doesn't start till you get there," barked Tuck, and off I went.

The sun broke through the clouds as I descended into the subway that wet October morning. I decided to get off the T at Park Street and walk across Boston Commons for some fresh air, and that's when I said aloud, to no one in particular, "What am I doing here?"

I knew all about the need to "uncake" our diamonds. But Boston, why did I come back to Boston? I knew the answer. It's not the troubles we experience in life that shape us, it's our response to the bitterness, pride, and regrets that consume us that determines whether we will "uncake" our diamonds.

I came back, I knew, because this is where I had lost my way.

And this is where I needed to uncake my diamond.

At the South End storefront, a dank, cluttered room, my boss, a guy with Thom McAn shoes and a lime green suit, waved me in.

"What's your name, kid?"

"Colin Patrick."

"Sit over there, Pat, while I find the Yellow Pages."

"The temp manager said you needed me to create a mailing list for a video on women runners."

"Bigger than that. I want a list of all the companies in Boston that do business with women."

"Who are we looking for?"

"We're not looking for anybody. We're making a mailing list. It's the Boston Marathon that's looking for the first girl."

"First girl?"

"Yeah, the 'Runner in Red' who ran the Boston Marathon in 1951. People think a girl snuck into the race back then. Some girl in a red hood. A sponsor paid the B.A.A. a ton of bucks for the right to

13

promote the 'Runner in Red' when he finds her."

"What's the B.A.A.?"

"The Boston Athletic Association, which conducts the race,*"* he said, as he found the phone book propping up a leg of the couch and gave a pull. "Until 1972 the B.A.A. didn't let girls into the Marathon. That's when old guys headed up the race committee. But the girls got tired of the old guys' crap and by the 1970s, they started fighting the sod busters."

"I thought you said a woman ran in 1951?"

"They don't *know* if one ran that early. That's why a sponsor, some bigwig business guy, paid the B.A.A. a ton of bucks for a sponsorship so he can make a big deal out of the 'Runner in Red.' He shelled out enough smackeroons, he must think he can find her."

"What do I do?"

"You make the mailing list so I can get the bigwig business guy to make a big deal out of me."

"Sounds to me like the bigwig business guy wants to bait women. What's his real deal?"

"Look, pal, I don't pay you to think, I pay you to stuff. So get working, OK? I got to go to a meeting."

With that he was gone, and I was leafing through the Yellow Pages trying to gauge which firms sold to women, when "Miracles" by Jefferson Starship played on the radio, and I thought of Bridget again, the idea of miracles, and it hit me how a song can pierce our shell of consciosness, when my boss banged his way through the door. "Shit," he said, and I watched him stand sideways against the window, shielding himself as he followed the movements of a man in a raincoat and a policeman across the street.

"Oh, Christ! My fuckin' luck," he said, as the man in the raincoat checked the addresses of storefronts.

"What?"

"Nothin.' Look, you never saw me, OK?"

With that he ran to the back of the room, searching for a way out, as across the street, the policeman and the man in the raincoat walked our way.

A moment later, the two were forced to pause to let a limo pass as a line of cars trailing the limo beeped their horns, and news vans and trucks with placards reading, "Finn for Governor," created an additional obstacle.

"Where's Sylvester?" the man in the raincoat asked me as he stepped through our door a moment later, while the policeman, a burly sort, stood behind him.

"Are you the B.A.A.?"

"DEA," he said, and my brain tried to sort it out, but all I could come up with was Drug Enforcement Administration.

"The DEA?"

"That's right. Who are you? Can I see some identification?"

I handed him my wallet, but as he studied the picture on my license I realized Sylvester—or whoever had disappeared out the back door—had more important worries than getting the mail out.

Before the man in the raincoat could ask another question, however, things got really strange, as a tiny, beady-eyed guy in a tattered coat walked up to our door whistling. The instant the dirty little guy saw the cop he turned and ran, while the cop—responding like a ball off a bat—bolted out the door behind him. Raincoat flapping, the DEA man chased after them, and I stepped out onto the sidewalk to watch, confused as hell.

It was the shots that got everyone's attention.

Two shots rang out as pedestrians ducked behind mailboxes, mothers with carriages screamed, and the press hopped from their TV vans with cameras and a new focus greater than covering the governor's campaign. Meanwhile, up the street in the center of the intersection, the dirty little guy lay spread-eagle in the street while the cop, whom he had fired off a round at, stood over him with a gun to his head.

"What was that all about?" I asked several men in business suits

15

who rushed down from their offices to join the throng on the street, held back now by police reinforcements.

"Drugs," said a thin man.

"Must be that new ring from Central America. Did you see the big story in the paper Sunday?"

"No, what story?" said a guy with a snub nose. "I didn't see the paper."

I listened as the thin man told how some government officials in El Salvador, former army generals, were working in partnership with a drug cartel to expand their operation into the US.

"How do you know this is that?" said Snub Nose.

"I overheard *him* talking," the thin one said, and he pointed to the DEA leader who stood in the middle of the street coordinating the local police as they frisked the dirty little guy and hustled him into a cop car.

"Unbelievable," said Snub Nose. "No sooner do the Feds shut down Florida than up pops Central America."

Suddenly the DEA leader walked toward me, motioning for me to join him in a tan sedan sitting at the curb.

"Me?" I said, mouthing the word, and he nodded.

Bald, muscular, in his 40s, he said his name was Clinton ("like the President, but different party, different worldview"). He questioned me for more than an hour, taking notes about my whole life, but it was the baseball that finally convinced him I was straight.

"I saw you play. At Fenway. You could go in the hole and get 'em, couldn't you?"

"Yeah."

"What happened?"

I told him about my ankle.

"Damn poor luck, ain't it?" he said, as his partner—the cop who had ducked the shot—held up a cell phone. Clinton looked at me, his face very serious. "Word to the wise. Don't go poking your nose into this kinda business, I don't care how down you think you might get."

"Don't worry," I said, but before he climbed out of the car to take the call, he said, "You're Kenny Patrick's kid brother, aren't you?"

"Yeah."

"I remember Kenny had a brother in baseball."

"Yeah," I said, surprised that someone from Boston knew Kenny who was a New York cop, a good one.

"I palled with Kenny in the Marines. He's a solid citizen, your brother."

"The best."

"I'm sure you miss being in the action. But keep your nose clean, kid, ya hear?"

I continued to hang around and watch after he drove off. In fact, I was the last to leave before police cleared the intersection. Most of all I couldn't take my eyes off the TV van and the cameraman. Clinton had nailed it!

Oh, to be in the middle of the action again!

It was then that I reached into my pocket for my wallet and found the scrap of paper Bridget had given me.

The one with Stan the news director's phone number.

CHAPTER THREE

I t was a bright blue spring day on Long Island, New York, the day of the accident.

I was nine and I had a ball game that evening. My mother had chores for me to do after school, make-work kind of stuff, things that would make me late for my game. I complained, but she insisted I do every last task before leaving for the ballpark on my bike.

I blamed her, saying it was her fault I was going to miss batting practice. I kept pestering her for a ride until finally, she relented, and I grabbed my cleats. They were muddy from a game earlier that week, and I set them on the dashboard to show her how mad I was that she had made me late.

As we drove she asked me nicely to take my dirty shoes off the dash, but I said I had no place to put them, and that's when she leaned over to slap them off.

"I told you to do something, young man," she said, as we passed through an intersection at Old Country Road and Jerusalem Avenue. An airline mechanic returning home from JFK had fallen asleep at the wheel, and he ran the light. He barreled into us, hitting us hard on my mom's side at 50 mph, according to the police report later.

I saw my mom's face one last instant as the car on her side crumbled like a kid balling foil from a pack of baseball cards.

For three months after that I didn't talk, even after I came out of a coma, since there was nothing I could do to make it better, to

18

undo what I had done, and I didn't want to talk to anyone again, ever.

"It was an accident," Kenny said, and I was grateful that he never blamed me for shattering our family. He even gave up his wrestling scholarship at Villanova in Pennsylvania to come home and be close for me.

But I didn't believe him that it wasn't my fault, and I have never believed anyone that I wasn't to blame for putting my goddamn shoes on the dash.

The receptionist at Channel 6 in Needham outside Boston told me Stan was busy, but he'd see me after his conference call ended.

"You can sit in the lounge and watch TV while you wait," she said, pointing to a room off to the side.

I sat down to watch as a segment called "Lead up to the New Millennium: A Women's History of the Boston Marathon," played on the station's waiting room TV. About 1,000 runners, all men, lined up in the street in Hopkinton for the start of the race in 1971 as half a dozen women lined up for photographers.

"It had been four years since Jock Semple chased Kathrine Switzer down the road in the 1967 Boston Marathon, calling worldwide attention to the issue of women's exclusion from the Boston Marathon," said a commentator. "But by 1971 women still were not permitted to run, and six young ladies have come to the start today to show their displeasure with the rules and run in the race, including the race co-director's daughter."

I watched as the gun went off and a duel developed in the race between Pat McMahon of Boston and Alvaro Mejia of Mexico, but at intervals the video cut to the six women sprinkled among the field and to one in particular, a blonde women with a Boston College singlet leading the women's contingent.

Then down the final straightaway came Mejia who had pulled ahead of McMahon and he raised his arms in triumph. But that shot cut quickly to the broader field and to a shot of the blonde woman from Boston College as she opened her lead on the other women in the final miles on Beacon Street. The film showed her barreling down the straight-away toward the finish line as the commentator and the crowd went wild, "Here comes Gallagher, the race director's daughter, she's on pace to break the women's world record for the marathon, unofficially of course since women are not allowed to participate formally. But nevertheless she is pouring it on, in a time close to three hours, faster than any woman has ever run a marathon, and uh-oh, here comes her father, Pop Gallagher, the race co-director. He's on record saying he won't allow a breach of the rules and he's moving to a place in front of the finish line. Oh, boy, looks like we may get a confrontation, since everyone knows Pop Gallagher will protect the integrity of the Boston Marathon...."

At that moment, Stan the news director, came into the lounge. I assumed he was Stan, because he said, "Are you Colin Patrick, the kid who wants to see me?" I nodded as I continued to watch the video with the blonde coed steaming toward the finish when all of a sudden, Pop Gallagher jumped into the street in front of his daughter, and waved his arms to block her.

"Bridget Maloney gave me your name," I said, one eye on the TV. "She said I could see you for a job."

"You know Bridget well?"

"I worked for her for six months as her cameraman in Philly."

"You know her well and you don't recognize her?"

"Huh?

"That's Bridget," he said, pointing to the TV. "And that's her father blocking her at the finish line of the 1971 Boston Marathon. It's a fairly famous shot in running circles. I trust you're a better cameraman than you are a sports historian."

OMG! I didn't say the words, but my face showed the shock. I stepped closer to the screen for a better look as Bridget squared off, her face inches away from the sour-faced curmudgeon who blocked her, and it *WAS* her. That was *Bridget!*

"Oh, my God!" I said, and Stan smiled.

"Come this way. You can tell me about all the other close friends you have."

I followed him to his office, but I walked backward so I could watch the screen and watch as Bridget, *MY* Bridget, melted under the glare of her father, Pop Gallagher, and stepped away from the finish line before crossing it, failing to finish the race in 1971.

Stan was a tall, stocky African-American, a guy I pegged for a linebacker in high school by the size of him. But what got me were his eyes: they were clear and bright and they held my gaze without wavering. He had outtakes from the video of the 1971 marathon, and he gave me the full background on Bridget, showing her running with the track team from Boston College to practice for her Boston Marathon run. The clips showed her practicing on the track with two guys, one identified by Stan as Jack Maloney, who Stan said was her estranged husband, and a guy who looked vaguely familiar.

"I know that guy," I said, meaning the one who was not her estranged husband. "I think I do anyway."

"You should, if you worked in Philly. That was your boss, the station owner, Steve Roman."

I offered another OMG face as I failed to make the connection between the huge portrait of Steve Roman in the news station lobby in Philadelphia and this shot of a trim, young guy—a top runner—in the 1971 video clip.

"If I hire you, as you tell me Bridget wants me to, he'll be your boss here as well."

I saved the OMG face, but said, "What?"

Stan told me how Roman had made a fortune on Wall Street and was buying up television stations, starting with two, one in Philly and the other in Boston, "Including this one, Channel 6. He has a pattern. He likes to own stations where Bridget works."

"I don't understand."

"Roman owns a marketing company that bought a sponsorship from the Boston Marathon as part of celebrating the new Millennium at this year's race. He wants our station to lead the search for the Runner in Red and he wants Bridget to come up from Philly to lead the project."

"When's she coming?"

"In a week. She's in NY now with Roman planning strategy to find the Runner in Red and make a big PR splash out of it."

The confusion showed on my face as he muttered, "Ah, neophytes," then he grabbed his clicker for the TV screen on the wall across from his desk.

"Let me show you a little history. You look like you're new to school."

"I'm baseball. I don't know anything about running."

"Obviously."

He showed clips from a Boston Marathon with the date "1966" stamped across the top. It showed a woman, "Roberta Gibb," as identified on the screen, running among the men and crossing the finish line in 1966 in 3 hours and 21 minutes.

"Bobbi Gibb was the first woman to complete the Boston Marathon. She snuck into the race in 1966 and beat more than two-thirds of the men's field. The media went crazy. There's a story about a reporter from the *Herald* who felt he was giving up Pulitzer Prize material when his editor had him tank his prose on Kenji Kenimara, the men's winner, to write a story on Gibb."

"Why weren't women allowed to run?"

"Amateur Athletic Union rules that governed the sport suggested women could hurt themselves if they ran more than 200 meters. That was the world back then. The Boston Marathon had to operate under those rules or lose the AAU sanction."

The next clip, "1967" showed a young woman in grey sweats, identified as "Kathrine Switzer," being pursued by a burly man who hopped off the press bus to chase her down the road.

"Who's that guy?"

"That's Jock Semple. He and Pop Gallagher were running rivals in the 30s and 40s. They became co-directors of the Boston Marathon in the 50s, and oversaw the race together. Jock passed away in 1988, but Pop was a bit younger and he's still around. He's in his 80s today, but he was stripped of his title as co-director after his skirmish with Bridget in 1971."

Again Stan put the scene up on the TV, the one with Pop Gallagher and Bridget squaring off eyeball to eyeball at the finish line.

"They canned Pop in 1971, why didn't they can Jock in 1967 for what he did to Switzer?"

"Jock made himself public enemy number one with the female gender in '67, that's for sure. But he was smart, too. He repented and he embraced women's running after his confrontation with Switzer. He became a strong advocate for women, and he even took to training top women runners, such as Patti Catalano. Women embraced Jock, including Kathrine Switzer. Pop on the other hand never made his peace, though he does train high school kids today. He has softened, I think, and a lot of people love him for all the good he did for the marathon over the years. But he never made peace with Bridget, and she never made peace with him."

I shook my head, trying to absorb it all.

"So there you have it. Bobbi Gibb and Kathrine Switzer broke the ice for women runners in the mid-60s, but if Bridget can prove that a woman ran in 1951, fifteen years before Bobbi Gibb, that will call for a total rewrite of women's running history. That's what Roman wants, he wants us to cross the finish line first on that story."

"Can you play the scene again? The one where Bridget approaches the finish line and Pop jumps in front of her in the '71 race."

"Sure," he said.

"What did Pop say to her?"

"What do you mean?"

"Play it again, take a closer look," I said, and he played the scene two or three more times, with the shot of Bridget barreling toward the finish, about to cross the line, when three feet short of the line Pop leans in front of her and has words. Whatever words they were, they froze Bridget more than his flailing arms did, and she recoils, not from the windmill of his arms, but from his words.

"Wow, you're right," Stan said. "He does say something to her. I never noticed. I'll ask her when she gets here. When I ask her what she wants me to do with you."

"Do with me?"

He held up the slip of paper with his name on it, the one Bridget had given me in Philly, the one I had passed onto the receptionist for Stan.

"Obviously she wants me to hire you. But for what? I assume to help her with Runner in Red, but give me a call next week and I'll get you an answer."

My head was spinning!

Bridget was not just a runner, but a champion runner. A Boston Marathon historical figure, a freakin' radical focused on breaking the gender barrier with Gibb, Switzer and other women pioneers. And taking on her father to do it! Now she was focused on the Runner in Red, a hunt for the first woman who quite possibly ran the Boston

Marathon fifteen years before history knew there had been a first female runner.

But why? For revenge? To show the world there was one woman her father *couldn't* stop?

I needed answers so I stopped at the Boston College library on Commonwealth Ave. on my way back to Boston. I learned that the Runner in Red was indeed a legend created after a group of Canadian runners in the 1951 Boston Marathon claimed they saw "a woman wearing red" running beside them during the marathon.

Their claim caused a great ruckus at the finish line in 1951 as reporters circled the Canadians for details. Had they been able to prove what they saw, the Runner in Red would have been the first woman to run a marathon on American soil. But Pop Gallagher, the race co-director, doused the flames of any scandal when he said the runner in red had been Tim Finn, a member of his Dorchester Athletic Association marathon team. Pop produced Tim at the finish line wearing a red sweatshirt with a red hood over his D.A.A. singlet and Tim—who had placed ninth in the race, securing victory for the D.A.A. team in the team category—said, "Yes, that was me wearing a red hood."

The Canadians continued to protest. They even took their claim to newspapers in Toronto, prolonging the story for a few more days, but Pop continued to insist the Runner in Red had been Finn and because "Pop was the staunchest champion of the rules God ever created," wrote the *Boston Globe's* Jerry Nason, the dean of Boston sportswriters, that did it.

The story never got legs, beyond becoming an urban legend.

I got in my car to head back to Dorchester after finishing at the library when I saw *her!*

She was a hundred feet down the road, and I hit the brakes. It had to be her: *blonde ponytail!*

She stood next to her disabled car on Commonwealth Ave. She had the car's hood up and I pulled in behind her and walked gingerly, thinking *ah, serendipity!*

That's what the world gives us when it wants to be kind.

"Trouble?" I said. I couldn't believe how gorgeous she was. Long and tall in tight fitting jeans, she wore a red t-shirt on that warm fall day. But all I focused on was her unmistakable trademark, her blonde ponytail. I had last seen that precious commodity flying back and forth across her shoulders in Philly as she had sped away from me and out of my life. Forever, as I had believed, until now!

"My car," she said. "It stopped, I don't know what to do."

"Here, let me take a look," I said, and I made "hmmm" sounds like a doctor examining a patient.

"Do you know what the problem is?"

"I do," I said, and I took a shot. "These old cars, like my sorry case back there," and I pointed to my car, which I had bought battered and bruised off a gas station parking lot after arriving in Boston. "Before the electronic ignition systems, these old cars worked off a set of points, which need to have a proper gap. I suspect the gap between your points collapsed."

She looked at me like I was speaking Greek, but all I could see were her blindingly brilliant blue eyes. I pulled out a parking ticket from my pocket, the one I had just gotten after overstaying my research in the library, and I used the thickness of the ticket to reconfigure the gap in her points, and *voila!* It worked.

I asked her to start her car again, and *presto*, it turned over. Through the windshield I could see a huge smile suffuse her face— directed at *ME!* I looked in the back seat of her car, at the countless boxes she had stacked back there.

"What's with all the baggage? You moving?"

"My mother just gave hell to my father again. I was staying there, but she's hopelessly cruel to him, and I'm going to Dorchester to live with my grandfather."

"Dorchester! That's where I live," I said, looking for any connection possible.

"Really, where in Dorchester?"

"I live above an entertainment establishment. Where does your grandfather live? Possibly I could follow you home to make sure your car doesn't break down again."

I saw the processing of that offer play out in her brain, but ultimately she decided I wasn't a stalker and she smiled. "That would be great, thank you!"

She scribbled on a piece of paper and handed the page to me: "Ellen Crutchfield. 183 Minot Street."

I took the paper, as horns blew and trumpets blared. It was like a Hallelujah chorus concert right there on Commonwealth Ave. in front of sandwich shops, auto dealer storefronts, and computer fix-it joints.

Just then a car pulled up, and pulled in behind mine.

"Ellen?" said a man in his 60s, a gray-haired hippy in a jeans jacket with his own ponytail, gunboat gray, under a ball cap. "You all right?"

By that, he meant "with *me.*"

"Yes," she said, beaming. "I called you. But you didn't need to come actually. This nice guy fixed my car, he said he'll follow me home."

"No need for that," said the aging hippy. "I'll take you in my car. Then I'll come back and get your car after I get you home safe."

He turned to me and said, "Thanks for your help," his tone perfunctory, hardly warm.

"No problem," I said, and several moments later blonde ponytail was pulling out of my life again, this time with an aging hippy.

Still, she offered me a smile and a cute wave out the passenger side window as the hippy's sedan sped away.

I watched her go and my spirits sank to a new depth, until I realized what I was holding in my hand and I beamed larger than I could ever remember smiling. I opened my hand and stared at the paper, with her fine delicate writing.

I had her address.

CHAPTER FOUR

I couldn't get the image of Ellen Crutchfield out of my head, the picture of her mesmerizing blue eyes as she smiled from behind the wheel of her car after *I* had made it start. I carried her image up the stairs to my apartment above the bar on Dorchester Avenue north of Fields Corner that evening and I was smiling until I checked my mail and saw the letter from my brother, Kenny.

"Hey, guy, haven't talked to you in a while," the note said, and I got a pit in my stomach, the way Kenny could be brusque when he meant to be affectionate. "We got the Mass of Remembrance for Dad at St. Patrick's in Huntington on Wednesday. It's the third anniversary of dad's passing and I know you won't miss the chance for a graveside visit, especially the way you still feel guilty about Mom."

I loved the guy, but oh his ham-handed way at connection-making!

Then I saw the PS and understood his real reason for the outreach: "I got something I need to talk to you about. An idea to help you turn your life around finally. Call me."

I had kept one thing from my playing days, my bat. I carried it in my duffle bag. A 31-ounce Louisville slugger, the bat had my initials, "C.P.," on the knob and pine tar on the handle from the day I got hurt.

The bat had traveled with me everywhere and I grabbed it after turning on the TV to watch the Red Sox. The Sox were doing well as they had earned a spot in the playoffs, and I assumed a position in an imaginary batter's box at the foot of my bed and stared hard at the Toronto southpaw as he looked in for the sign.

Moonlight bathed the floor of my tiny room as I locked eyes with the pitcher who curled into position, arm cocked, and I tightened my grip along the handle, waiting. I watched the ball as it left the pitcher's hand, and I leaned into the pitch, swinging hard with all my might and I turned on the ball, driving it deep into the night, out my window and over the huddled rooftops of Dorchester.

Gone.

A tape measure job.

"I'll turn my own life around, Kenny," I said as I rounded the bases in my mind. Then, as I put my bat back into the duffle bag, I said it again to myself and to the world beyond the rooftops.

"I'm going to find her again, damn it, and I'm going to make Ellen Crutchfield mine."

The next day at noon I went downstairs to the bar to work the lunch shift, part of my deal with the owner for a break on the rent, when two regulars pulled up seats. One guy they called "Moon Shot" because he had a moon face and drank shots with his Buds.

The other guy they called "Tiger" because he wore a Detroit Tigers cap, and he knew everything about Boston sports. I don't know why he wore a Detroit cap when he was such a Boston freak— something about a girl he dated from Detroit, the only girl who ever went out with him according to Moon Shot—and as such the hat was his connection to that sweet memory.

"What's with the pink case?" said Moon Shot as I set the pouch Ellen Crutchfield had dropped in Philly on the bar. "You played for the Sox, now you playing for the other team?"

"I'm going to give this back to the girl who lost it, after I finish liquoring you guys up," I said, and I showed Moon Shot and Tiger the contents from the case, including the gold medal with the embossed writing, *Boston Athletic Association, 1951.*

"That's the 1951 Boston Marathon gold medal. Where did you get it?" said Tiger.

"Belongs to a girl I met. I'm going to give it back to her." I pulled out the piece of paper Ellen had scribbled for me. "Know where 183 Minot Street is?"

"Head south on Dorchester Ave. 'til you get to the Ashmont T, the end of the Red Line. After the station, about quarter of a mile, you'll see Minot Street, make a left and head up the hill. But the medal is missing the diamond in the middle." Tiger pointed to an empty space, a hole above the Boston Athletic Association logo, a unicorn. "The Boston Marathon winner's medal has a diamond in the middle. That's what makes the Boston Marathon gold medal unique. But this one is missing the diamond. What's with that?"

"I don't know."

"Shineki Tanaka of Japan won the race in 1951. How did your girl get the medal won by Tanaka? Is she Japanese?"

"She's USA, a blonde. A drop dead gorgeous blonde."

"1951 was a big year for the Americans. In '51, for the first time since the war ended the Japanese sent a team to Boston. The Americans didn't have anyone to compete with Tanaka, but Jock Semple and Pop Gallagher saw a chance to carry the day for America by winning the team prize. Whoever won the team trophy, Jock's Boston Athletic Association team or Pop's Dorchester Athletic Association, could claim ownership defending the homeland against the Japs. That got Pop and Jock's juices going, know what I mean."

"Pop Gallagher? He was a crusty dude, I hear."

"Not in these parts. You're in Dorchester, boy. This is Pop Gallagher country."

Tiger waved me over to a wall with sports photos—Ted Williams, Bobby Orr, and other baseball and hockey photos—but with running pictures, too. He pointed to a photo of five crew cut boys standing with a middle-aged man. Stout as a fireplug, the middle-aged man stood with the boys and beamed as he held a trophy, tall as a skyscraper.

"That's Pop Gallagher with his Dorchester Athletic Association team after they won the team prize in 1951. Tanaka won the marathon, but Pop and his D.A.A. boys planted the flag for America. That's the only time Pop's D.A.A. team ever beat Jock Semple's Boston Athletic Association team. That was a huge win for Dorchester to be able to claim they beat the Japanese, especially with the war so fresh in everyone's mind."

I studied the photo of Pop and noted his barrel chest, the one he had used to block Bridget twenty years later. I noticed, too, that one of the boys, a short kid with big eyes, wore a sweatshirt with a hood. I remembered that the story at the BC library said the hood was red.

"Who's the guy with the red hood?"

"That's Tim Finn. Next to Tim is his brother Joe Finn, the Governor. He's running for re-election. This place uses Joe's posters instead of wallpaper." Tiger pointed to the "Elect Joe Finn, Dorchester's Own!" posters that plastered the place.

"Do you remember anything about the Runner in Red? A woman who ran in the Boston Marathon in 1951?"

"That's a rumor a group of Canadian runners dreamed up, but it's never been proven. The Canadians said they saw a woman in red running beside them during the race. Pop undercut that, though, by pointing to Tim Finn and his red hood. I wouldn't give it any credence. Pop's word was gold and the story never went anywhere."

I returned to the bar as Tiger followed me and offered a throwaway line. "Don't know how your gorgeous blonde got Tanaka's gold medal, but you better hope she doesn't think you stole her diamond."

Moon Shot piled on, as he tapped the pink case.

"Maybe you like diamonds, now that you play for the other team."

After my shift ended at three o'clock, I drove south from Fields Corner. It was stop/start on the narrow, traffic-clogged streets as I worked my way past parks with holes in the chain link fences and storefronts offering a mix of coffee shops, auto parts places, liquor stores, and law offices with Irish names on the signs. A hundred years earlier, Dorchester had once been an exclusive neighborhood, but now it was struggling, like a runner in the last stages of a marathon trying to hold on.

I made a left after the Ashmont T station and turned onto Minot Street as Tiger had directed. I continued past huddled houses, several with cars on cinder blocks in the driveways, yet some of the wooden clapboard houses retained tidy, cared-for looks, including the small house Blonde Ponytail stepped out of.

Blonde Ponytail!

Ellen Crutchfield wore blue shorts and a yellow top as she crossed the street in front of me twenty yards ahead. She started to jog and I gave it gas to catch up to her when a panel truck—R. J. Casey and Sons Electrical—pulled out from the curb and not only blocked me, but blocked my view of the girl.

I swung hard around the truck, but in the meantime, Blonde Ponytail had turned down a side street—I didn't see which one— and my heart raced as I tried to guess which turn to make. I made two rights and a left, clipping my tires on the curb each time, even prompting a woman walking her dog to hop back, but still I did not see Ellen, and then I came to a dead end.

"Damn it," I shouted as I backed up, tires screaming, along with my id, and before long I found myself back out on Minot Street, where I had started, hopelessly lost!

"God damned truck!"

I drove to the bottom of the hill past the house Ellen Cruchfield had stepped out of, anticipating that if she had turned right, most likely she was heading to the water—and I assumed I might find her there since my understanding of runners was they liked to run along paths near water.

Confused by all the intersecting streets, I felt like a soldier floundering in another guy's rice paddy as I worked my way east toward the harbor area. Ten minutes later I came down the back end of what signs told me was Savin Hill and I stopped at a red light in front of a long straight stretch of road, Morrissey Boulevard. The harbor waters rolled out in front of me and that's when I saw her, running along the shoulder of Morrissey Blvd. toward me from the right. I leaned on the horn and waved out the window to get her attention, but she regarded me with a mix of scorn and irritation, assuming I was a stalker, and she quickened her pace as she passed in front of my car and headed down Morrissey Blvd., gliding away now to the left.

I continued to wait for the light to change, like sitting through a 20 inning ballgame, and that's when I saw a red sedan come barreling down the boulevard from my right. It passed in front of me going 70 mph, easily, as the driver weaved through traffic, and I honked to warn her, but she never saw the car as it came up behind her and brushed her, or appeared to.

Over she went, head over heels down a ditch, and I ran the light to catch up as she did another cartwheel, then two more, and landed in a ravine in the water in front of the entrance to Columbia Point.

I pulled up onto the shoulder and raced down the embankment where I found her lying at the water's edge trembling.

"Hey," I said. "You OK?"

She sat up, eyes wide, hip deep in water, and I lifted her as she raised a fist in the direction of the red car and shouted, "Asshole!"

"Wow, that was close," I said, as I helped her stand on bandy legs, and I knew she was going to be OK, the way she was giving it to the the offending driver.

The sedan disappeared around a bend, and I picked wet leaves, cigarette butts, McDonald's wrappers and whatever else had been in the ditch off her legs and arms.

"I got hit once," she said, as I led her by the arm to my car.

"You what?"

"I got hit by a car once," she repeated, but she didn't fight me as I eased her into the front seat on the passenger side and I draped her shoulders with a blanket from my trunk.

"You got hit?"

"Who are you?" she said, before recognition flashed in her eyes.

"Oh!"

"I met you yesterday, remember? Your car broke down."

"What are you doing here?" she said, meaning *here*, in this place at this time.

"I was looking for you."

"Me?"

"I came to return something to you."

"What?"

I realized it would be too complicated to explain about Philly and her blowing me off the day I had put a camera in her face, so I figured I would tell her about the pink fanny pack later. I said simply, "Doesn't matter. Where can I bring you now?"

"Home," she said, and she pointed behind us.

"Right, your grandfather's house," and I turned the car around and headed back down Morrissey Blvd.

"How do you know that?"

"You told me," and I showed her the piece of paper she had given me the day before with her address.

"You know my name now too, don't you, smart guy?"

"Nice to meet you, Miss Crutchfield," I said with as a big a smile as I could muster, and it worked because she smiled back as color returned to her face.

She didn't say anything as we drove and she pointed out turns for me to take, then she said several minutes later, "What's your name?"

"Colin."

"And what do you do, Colin? That is, when you're not fishing girls out of Boston Harbor and fixing their cars?"

I blew past bartender as an answer and said, "I'm up for a position working on a Boston Marathon project."

"Oh, *that's* interesting," she said, and she pointed to the house that she had stepped out of earlier, before her run-in with the red sedan. "Why don't you park here and come in. I will only be a minute. Since you'll be working on the marathon, you may find the house interesting."

"What do you mean only a minute? Aren't you going to lie down or something?"

But she was already out of the car and walking toward the front door of the house. "I've got a month till the New York City Marathon and I'm 30 miles short for the week," she said over her shoulder. "I need to train."

"New York City Marathon? You're going to run in the New York City Marathon?"

"I plan to win it."

She held the front door open for me, and I followed her in. The place was dark with a heavy oak furniture theme, which combined with the thick drapes made the place feel even darker, but the walls were filled with running photos which gave the tiny place some life.

"Looks like a marathon museum," I said, as she disappeared into a bathroom off the kitchen, but before she closed the door she said, "I thought you'd find the place interesting since you'll be working for the marathon."

I talked to her through the bathroom door. "You think you can win the New York City Marathon?"

"Winning Boston next April is my real goal. My grandfather and I, we plan to use New York as a tune-up." A moment later she stepped out of the bathroom and caught me staring at her bare midriff, with her perfectly flat stomach. She wore a red sports bra and fresh new red shorts. "What are you looking at?"

I switched my eyes from her midriff, and pointed to a photo on the wall. It showed a tall, thin young woman with a blonde ponytail striding down a road in a Boston College singlet. "That you?"

She turned to face the wall and her blonde ponytail followed the snap of her head. "Yes, that's me at Boston College before I got hurt."

"You got hurt? You mean the car you told me about that hit you?"

"No, that was in Oregon, after I got married."

"You're married."

"I was. In college I ran in the Olympic Trials my sophomore year, but I got hurt. I was leading the race, until I got a stress fracture at mile 18 and hobbled in in 10th place. After that I lost my chance for shoe money, no shoe sponsor wanted a tenth place finisher, and that's when I got married."

"That's the Crutchfield?"

"More like a 'Ball-and-chain field.'"

"You're not married anymore?"

"It wasn't bliss."

"What happened?"

She was about to tell me when a key turned in the front door and the hippy with the gray ponytail, the guy who had taken her home after her car broke down, walked in with an old man who was short but who had a powerful frame. The old man had piercing blue eyes which he trained on me.

"You again?" said the guy with the gray ponytail, hardly congenial again.

"Tim," said Ellen. "This is Colin. He gave me a ride home after some asshole ran me off the road."

All of this was too much for gray ponytail to absorb and he shook his head confused as the old man continued to stare at me with a laser-like glare.

"Who are you?" said the old man pronouncing each word individually and with a voice as hard as steel.

"This is Colin," said Ellen. "I wanted him to see your house since he's going to work for the Boston Marathon."

"You work for the Marathon?" said gray ponytail. "Who for, the B.A.A.?"

"No, for a television station, actually."

This got everyone's attention, including Ellen's, and not in a good way.

"What television station?" said gray ponytail.

I wanted to impress. "I'll be working on a project at Channel 6 to find the first woman who ran the Boston Marathon. The Runner in Red, they call her."

I might as well have dropped a fucking bomb.

"You work with my mother?" said Ellen, and white showed on all four sides of her eyes.

Now it was my turn to show an OMG face. "Your mother…" and I fumbled for the words as images flashed through my mind, pictures crystal clear of her mother and my connection to her. "Your mother is Bridget?"

"Why didn't you *tell* me you worked with my mother?" said Ellen, and I could see pain, shock, hurt, surprise—most of all disdain for me—in her eyes.

"Out!" I don't know who said it, the old man or gray ponytail, but it was gray ponytail who leaned his shoulder into me—like a bobcat machine on a construction site—and began moving me toward the door.

"Don't hurt him," I heard Ellen say, which I was grateful for, but the next thing I knew I was all alone on the front stoop, and I heard the door slam behind me. *Bang!*

I don't know how long I stood on the stoop with my head ringing, as if someone had placed a kettle bell over me and whacked it. I lost and any ability to think clearly. The next thing I knew I was standing at my car, unaware of the steps I had taken to get to the car from the house.

Then I remembered the pink pouch and the reason I had come.

I returned to the porch and rang the ball, about a hundred million times, before Ellen's face, still reflecting hurt and shock, appeared in a window beside the door.

I held up the pouch, to show her, and I could see her process that, but at some point she motioned to me to set the pouch on the stoop and leave it there.

That's what I remember most, her motion with her finger to leave the pouch on the porch, and the words that followed as I read her lips:

"Then you go away!"

CHAPTER FIVE

Tiger knocked on my door a few minutes after I got back to my apartment.

"Your Boston Marathon medal got me really interested and I wanted to know more. I found this," he said, and he handed me pages he had copied from a seven-year-old edition of *Sports Illustrated.*

The story was titled, "Like Mother/Like Daughter."

"Where did you get this?"

"Boston Public Library. They've got tons of old stuff."

The story had been written while Ellen was a senior in high school. It told how she had broken the American schoolgirl record for the mile, prompting twenty colleges to pursue her, but she chose Boston College. "I want to follow in my mother's footsteps," she said in the story below a photo showing Ellen and Bridget smiling on the track at BC.

"See the name?" Tiger said.

"Ellen Maloney."

"Pre-Crutchfield."

"In the days when mother and daughter still talked to each other," I said and I grabbed my coat.

"Where are you going?"

"To Boston Public Library. To do *my* homework."

I had questions. The *Sports Illustrated* story told how in high school Ellen had idolized her mother and wanted to be like her. She chose Boston College, Bridget's school, over twenty other colleges. Now she was not only training under Pop's tutelage, she was living at his house.

What had prompted Ellen to switch allegiances?

Most importantly I wanted to know why the Runner in Red was so critical to Bridget that she would choose to pursue a mystery figure and jeopardize her family?

When I had helped her with her car Ellen told me her mom had given her dad "hell." I thought Bridget was estranged from her husband. Were they back together and where did the husband come down on the Ellen/Bridget/Pop triangle?

At the library I found *Time* and *Newsweek* from April, 1971. Both had stories on the "Boston Marathon Stand-off," as they called the finish line incident between Bridget and Pop Gallagher a quarter of a century earlier.

Reading the old clips interested me, not only for the dated look of the clothes, or the cheap prices of items in the black and white ads, or even the corny copy of the ads themselves ("I can't believe I ate the WHOLE thing!"), but for the tenor of the times which appeared to value men over women, without pretense or shame.

Both *Time* and *Newsweek* told how Bridget had gotten into running despite the resistance, i.e., rules created by men that kept women from competing in races such as the Boston Marathon. Bridget's teacher, a nun named Sister Josephine, had formed a union with Bridget to resist, according to the story, with the nun even helping Bridget adapt a pair of men's track shoes.

Those were the days before shoe companies made running shoes for women, so the two crammed tissue paper into the toe box of a pair of men's flats. They made them fit so Bridget could run the roads with two male friends, Jack Maloney and Steve Roman, top runners at Boston College High School. The sight of a girl in short pants running along the roads was unfamiliar, and Bridget was taunted by male drivers who hollered out their windows, "What are you runnin' for, to catch a husband?"

Mrs. Gallagher, taking a cue from Pop, was also upset by her daughter's running, according to the story. "You'll get big, unsightly muscles," Bridget quoted Mrs. Gallagher saying. "Nobody will want to marry you."

A doctor at Peter Bent Brigham testified that running was unhealthy for women. "Running distances greater than 200 meters could inhibit their ability to procreate," he said, bluntly.

But the real rub was with Pop, who accused Bridget of bringing shame on his family with her "wanton disregard for the rules." It was easy, the articles hinted, to see how this father/daughter relationship was a powder keg waiting to explode, and it did just that at the finish line of the 1971 Boston Marathon.

Still, I didn't understand: if Pop had opposed Bridget, why was he training Ellen to win the race? And why had she accepted his help?

Was Pop's interest in Ellen strategic, his way to get back at her mother for embarrassing him in 1971? If so, why was Ellen complicit? And the Runner in Red? Was that Bridget's strategy, her attempt to embarrass her father to show how the rule enforcer had been inept at enforcing the rules as early as 1951?

I couldn't figure it out, so I kept digging.

The librarian directed me to the microfiche room, where I found copies of the *Boston Globe* dating back to the 1890s. I started with the first Boston Marathon, April 15, 1897, eager to gain an understanding of the early runners and what drove them, especially Pop Gallagher.

Fifteen runners trudged over dirt roads in 1897 in the initial Boston Marathon. Tiger had been right, most of the runners were rough-hewn types, laborers and such. I read through countless stories of the early years, including 1917, when "Bricklayer" Bill Kennedy—who took Pop under his wing after Pop emigrated from

Ireland as a 17-year-old in 1932—won the gold medal after sleeping on a pool table in the South End.

I sensed a special camaraderie among these "plodders," as they were called. Ridiculed by the general population for the countless hours they spent training on often deserted roads, each generation appeared to take it upon themselves to pass the mantle to the next, preserving all that had come before. That's why Pop had committed himself so strongly to his Dorchester Club, I guessed, and that's why Jock Semple—Pop's chief rival during their years on the roads— had given just as selflessly to create his own marathon club, the "B.A.A. boys." The two plodders had competed vigorously during the 30s and 40s, and now they continued their head-to-head competition through their young surrogates during the 1950s.

Pop and Jock's dedication to their clubs represented an extension of the rivalry that had given their lives definition when they were young. Later, dutiful servants to the traditions of the race, they fulfilled their responsibility by mentoring boys who followed them into the sport. It was here, I realized, that Bridget posed a threat: she was not a *boy!* She and the other women who wished to run in the mid-1960s challenged everything the old guard had worked so hard to establish and now struggled just as hard to preserve.

A line from the 1971 *Time* article resonated with me: "There's no place for a woman in this," Pop had said in explaining his opposition to his daughter, but now I understood the full meaning of his quote: *women belonged on the sidelines. Men owned the thick of things. Women transgressed when they presumed equality and pressured for inclusion in the action.*

In Pop's mind stepping across the line to block Bridget in 1971 was simply an extension of his philosophy on the nature of the world and how it worked.

"Rules"—and insisting on the observance of them—served as a convenient vehicle to ensure that the structure be sustained. Suddenly I saw the 1971 "stand-off" in a fresh light. Bridget and

Pop's conflict served as the perfect dramatic setting for the clash of ideals that had surged to the surface on so many fronts during the turbulent 60s and came to a head by 1971 with Bridget and Pop.

This is what Pop had been protecting. It was a sentiment as faded and dated as the pages of the old periodicals themselves: his was a resentment for women who overstepped. "Interlopers," he had called them, those who threatened the order of the world that had formed him.

I came to the library to pursue my attraction to Ellen, the daughter, but I became more deeply intrigued by Bridget, her mother, my friend and mentor, the person who had given me a helping hand in Philadelphia when I had been at my lowest ebb.

I was intrigued by Bridget, a woman of countless conflicting drives, because of her personal investment in me but also because her struggle—to turn a concept such as the Runner in Red into something real—was not unlike my own struggle to find a patch of ground I could stand on to call my own.

But Ellen continued to confuse me. Why was Ellen, a woman who benefited from the pioneering efforts of her mother, so opposed to Bridget—and why was Ellen siding with the man who had not only blocked Bridget at the finish line but had opposed his daughter her whole life for no other reason than that she was a woman?

The next morning I went to Channel 6 to see Stan, thinking maybe he could shed light, but instead he greeted me with "You're hired. Bridget called yesterday. She wants you to be her cameraman on the Runner in Red project."

"Can I see her?"

"She'll be up from New York soon. You said you wanted to be back in the middle of the action. Well, son, game's on for you now."

He signaled me to follow him to his car and we drove out to a firehouse at the corner of Route 16 and Commonwealth Ave. in Newton, the 17-mile mark in the Boston Marathon.

We got out of his car and he motioned to me to follow him as he walked up Commonwealth Ave. "This is the start of Heartbreak Hill," he said. "The race presents the runners with three consecutive rises over the next three miles, from here up to Boston College. This stretch of Commonwealth Ave., this is where your focus will be when you work with Bridget. This is where the Canadian runners insisted they saw the Runner in Red."

"Can I ask you a question?" I said. "This whole thing, finding a woman who may or may not exist. I understand what Bridget gains in a political sense if she proves the legend true—she gives women a new hero. I get it, but I met Bridget's daughter and the project is pitting mother against daughter. What's the real motivation for Bridget? Is this all about making a political statement, or is it revenge, a desire by Bridget to stick it to Pop Gallagher for something he did to her in 1971? And why would Bridget risk her relationship with her daughter for that?"

Stan smiled. "If you know Bridget there's one thing true about her, she's an adamantine personality."

"Meaning?"

"She *never* gives up when truth is the issue."

"You've known her a long time?"

"Since we were kids in Dorchester and hopped fences as the cops chased us after we pilfered goods from Baker's Chocolate. She was a fast runner even then." He smiled, and I could see in his eyes the deep affection he had for Bridget. "She's all about story, son. Give her a storyline and she will stop at nothing to get to the bottom of it. I remember a time when she was in high school. There was a nun— Sister Josephine. I remember the nun's name because Bridget talked so much about the support she got from her teacher. Sister Josephine balanced out all the deficits Bridget faced living under Pop's roof.

"One day Sister gave the class an assignment to write an essay

45

advocating a point of view. Bridget picked running. She tried to get Pop for an interview, but Pop refused. Not to be deterred Bridget took the T into town to Boston Garden where she showed up at Jock Semple's physiotherapy clinic. Semple was training a group of his B.A.A. runners and she asked him point blank why women couldn't run in the Boston Marathon. He said, 'Because it's against the rules,' but Bridget kept pestering him for a 'real reason.' Johnny Kelley, Semple's top runner for the B.A.A., and Tim Horgan, a *Herald* sports reporter, took her aside and brought her downstairs for coffee. Horgan told her, 'Let me see what you come up with.' He liked her story so much he had the *Herald* run her essay, "Why Can't Jane Run?" on the front page.

"Pop was livid, of course, and I suspect she paid dearly at home in terms of the silent treatment. But this was the 60s, when Roberta Gibb, Kathrine Switzer and Sara Mae Berman and others were coming to the fore. So fighting for a cause has always been a central theme for Bridget. I'm not surprised that she would want a definitive answer on the Runner in Red, to know whether the legend is true or not. But I do think Roman may see things differently.'"

Stan told me how Roman and Jack Maloney, Bridget's estranged husband, shared a special bond with Bridget. Jack Maloney and Roman were best friends at Boston College High School. After Bridget's story appeared in the *Herald*, Jack showed up at Bridget's school and said, "Jane can run with me." She started training with him, doing workouts on the B. C. High track, and he introduced her to Roman. Jack and Roman were the city's top high school milers and training with them got her into great shape. By the time the three of them got to Boston College, Bridget took up with Roman. "It didn't end well," Stan said.

"What happened?"

"I don't know the details, but in the end, Bridget married Jack while Roman went off to Wall Street."

"So you think the Runner in Red is a play by Roman to get Bridget back?"

"He keeps buying TV stations where she works. And he's paid a lot of dough to buy a sponsorship at the Marathon to celebrate the Runner in Red on the chance they find her. But I doubt his interest is community advancement, or even the advancement of women's running. He bought another company, one that makes running shoes, with a shoe called 'Women First.' Roman is all about making money, and he doesn't care if he has to use people to do that, even a former paramour."

"You think he's using Bridget so he can sell shoes after she finds the Runner in Red for him? After that, though, then what?"

"Roman is still in a race with Jack Maloney, if you ask me. Throughout their running careers Roman never lost a race to Jack."

"Except the most important one."

"I think you're on the right track with your question, kid."

As I parked at the curb in front of my place in Dorchester, my cell phone rang, but I didn't recognize the 617 number.

"Colin?" the voice said on the other end.

"Bridget?"

"How's my bridge-burner? Stan taking good care of you?"

"I've got to talk to you, Bridget."

"Good idea. Let's go inside."

"Where are you?"

"In a parking space across the street."

I turned and saw that unmistakable smile as she sat behind the wheel of her parked car, her phone to her ear.

"How did you know where I lived?"

"I'm an investigative reporter, remember? Plus you filled out a job application," she said, but by the time she finished her sentence she was standing at my driver's side window. "Come on, sweetie, let's talk. Time's a wastin.'"

Rather than go upstairs to my apartment she suggested we get a table at the tavern. "I need a beer," she said.

Moon Shot didn't recognize her, but Tiger did and his eyes opened wide at having a celebrity in the place. We found a quiet spot at the back of the room and Bridget said, "Who wants the first question?"

"Me," I said. "Why are you risking your relationship with Ellen to find the Runner in Red?"

"Wow, that's an awfully big opening line."

'Why is the Runner in Red more important to you than your daughter?"

"First, let me say I love Ellen more than you or anyone can know. Let me leave it at that for the moment, OK?"

"Are you looking to get back at your father because he stopped you at the finish line in 1971?"

"My, you have educated yourself in the few weeks since Philadelphia."

"Tell me straight, Bridget, or I'm going upstairs and this is over. Do you hate your father so thoroughly that you'd risk losing your daughter?"

"Hate? That's a strong word."

"He stopped you at the finish line."

"Let me get two beers," she said, and she went to the bar. Tiger who could talk the paint off a wall became shy as a freshman at a college mixer as Bridget stood beside him and ordered two pints. She set mine in front of me, and took a long hit on hers before continuing.

"I oppose him to my core. That's more precise." I watched as shadows appeared below her eyes and lines marred her face. "My disdain for Pop—that's a more accurate word—and my desire to find the Runner in Red are the same thing. I have never told anybody this. Not even Jack, whom I've known since I was fifteen."

"You're back with your husband?"

"In a manner of speaking. But he supports Pop training Ellen and that puts us in opposition. But that's a topic for another conversation, another day."

"Why did you run in '71? Were you trying to get Pop to oppose you."

"I ran because I had promised my teacher."

"Your teacher?"

"Sister Josephine, my nun in high school. You once told me your brother watched out for you. I had Sister Josephine. She encouraged me during my darkest days with Pop."

"Were you trying to get Pop to block you, to draw him out?"

She smiled, a faint one. "He always blocked me. It didn't matter what the occasion was. It was like I was a bad seed to him my whole life. That's how he made me feel. He never once smiled at me. Never once patted me on the back. No affection. Ever." She took another hit on her beer. "Even when I tried to reach out, when I was a young girl, all he cared about were his boys. They were his life. Every Sunday, his boys and his road races. I thought maybe that's how I could get close to him. One Sunday I offered to ride in the car with him and give out sponges during a road race. But when I reached out the car window to give a sponge to Johnny Kelley, from Jock's B.A.A. team, Pop slapped my hand. 'Dammit, girl,' he shouted. 'Kelley's a Semple man!' Every time I tried to climb under a corner of the tent and enter his world he shut me out.

"But I loved running because of Sister Josephine. She took me to the Boston Marathon in 1957. I was five, but I remember how we stood at the finish line. I was just tall enough to look over the rope and I watched as Johnny Kelley—Young John—came speeding down the final straightaway on Exeter Street. Pop had forbidden me to go to the finish line, where he said I would be in the way of the men who did the work, but Sister—a friend of the family—took me without his knowledge and I was swept up in all the pageantry. As I watched Young John float down those last few yards, his eyes wide and the crowd roaring, I decided I wanted to be a runner, too."

"But Pop blocked you?"

"At every turn."

"But he's not that way with Ellen."

"It's terrible what he did to her before the Olympic Trials, the workouts he gave her. It was a regime too rigorous for her at that point in her development. I tried to tell her, but she blew me off and sure enough she got hurt and failed in the race. She hit the skids after her loss and married that empty suit."

"Crutchfield?

"A real zero. I tried to warn her, but she married him anyway. Then after that fell apart, she moved to Oregon, where things really went off the track."

"Now she's back in Boston."

"Yes, preparing for a comeback, but I feel like Pop is stealing my daughter. He's giving her workouts way too stressful again. It's the same movie and she will pay the price." She looked at me and I could see all the way to the back of her blue eyes, the pain back there.

"Is that why you want to find the Runner in Red, to embarrass Pop and pressure him to stop training Ellen?"

"That and because he hurt me more powerfully than I've ever been hurt."

"Oh?"

"Jack and Steve were both top collegiate milers at Boston College, but they wanted to try the Boston Marathon in 1971. It was Jack who gave me the idea to run the race and go for a women's world record as a way to pressure the B.A.A. to change the rules and allow women to compete. The women's world record was 3:02:53, held by Caroline Walker. As I approached the finish line I was exhausted, but I was exhilarated, too, knowing that I had come the whole way and I was on pace for the world record. Jack got fourth that day and stood behind the line cheering me on, while Roman, who got third, was off somewhere giving an interview. Then Pop appeared suddenly, waving his arms and shouting, 'Get out!'"

"What did you do?"

"We stood face to face, as you know, all the photos show that, and I said, 'What will you do if I don't?' And he said, 'Don't make me.'"

"He said that?"

"I said, 'What will you do, disown me?' and he said the words I will never forget, he said, 'That won't be necessary because you're not my daughter anyway.'"

"What?"

"I never told anybody this, but that's how I learned I was adopted, Colin, standing three feet short of the finish line at the Boston Marathon in 1971."

"I can't believe it. He said that to you?"

"It worked, because I stepped off the road. I was crushed. I failed to finish that day, but I decided three things. First, I decided I would never give in to anyone again, ever. Secondly, I decided I would erase all traces of Pop Gallagher from my life, and third—most importantly—I decided I would find my mother."

"Your mother?"

"Yes. My birth mother, because until I find my real mother I'm Pop Gallagher's daughter, a member of his family. I won't be complete until I can look into my mother's eyes and ask her why she abandoned me to be raised in a house with a man like that. Until I find my real mother, I will continue to live with a huge hole in my heart."

I watched her, half expecting a tear, not knowing what to expect, but there are no tears with Bridget and she said in an even tone, "So, there you have it."

"And the Runner in Red?"

"The Runner in Red is important to me, Colin, because I believe she is my mother."

"What?"

"That's right. Roman has convinced me."

"How?"

"He's sending his son to the station next week with a man who claims to have proof."

"Junior is coming to town?"

"He's going to be the assignment editor at Channel 6 for the Runner in Red project. Some things we have to endure for a greater good."

"I can't take this job, Bridget, if that's the case."

"I need you, Colin."

"You don't need *them*. You can find the Runner in Red on your own."

"Actually, Roman is critical. He has the resources to get the information we'll need. We need Roman."

"He's using you, Bridget, He's got a shoe company. Stan told me. They make shoes called 'Women First.' He'll let you find the Runner in Red, and he'll make a ton of money off that, then flip the company. The same way he'll flip you once you give him what he needs."

"By then I'll have what I need. I will know who my mother is. But I can't do this alone, Colin. I need you, someone loyal who does not bend and will not break."

"Ellen. That's what I want, Bridget. I want to know your daughter better. But if I work with you, no way will she give me a chance."

"You lost your mother, Colin. I have never had a mother."

"How did you find that out about me?"

"After you nailed Junior at the Haverford School, I did my research. Oh, by the way, I never let Junior put that little boy on the air."

"That's good to know."

"I need you, Colin. Say yes, please."

I sat a long time without talking. How could I mend fences with Ellen if I said yes to Bridget? But I could hear Bridget's desperate plea, her need to find her mother, and I found myself responding to that, to a call from a woman in motion. Possibly I could do both. Possibly I could help Bridget find the Runner in Red and get to know Ellen better at the same time.

Making unconventional choices was not new to me, and certainly, I wasn't afraid to take a chance. If you want to be an eagle you've got to fly like one, that was still my mantra. But I did hedge my bet.

"On one condition," I said.

"Whatever you want, tell me."

"Never lie to me again."

"I never lied to you."

"You set me up, Bridget. You gave me Stan's number that day in Philadelphia to set it up so I would be in Boston when you needed me."

"I saved you in Philly after you got off that bus, remember that?"

"You're my strongest supporter and I want to support you, Bridget. But never play me for a mark again. Promise me."

"I need you, Colin. There is no one else I would ask except you. But I hear you, and I promise I will never put you in a compromising position again. Will you run with me?"

She raised her glass to clink with mine, at the same moment Tiger appeared at the table to ask for her autograph.

I worried that I might never succeed with her daughter, but I was satisfied that I was making the right call with Bridget. I clinked glasses with her, though I knew I was agreeing to be Bridget's boy again.

I thought to myself, *here you go again, kid, just like the day you chose to give up a scholarship to Notre Dame for a chance to play baseball.*

The castle or the outhouse, no in between, as my dad used to say.

CHAPTER SIX

r. Pat O'Neill, my dad's cousin, led the prayer ceremony for my father at Holy Rood Cemetery on Long Island Wednesday after a Mass of Remembrance earlier that day. I had not been home since my father's death from cancer three years earlier, but as I stood at the gravesite beside Kenny and his wife, Rosemary, I felt a familiar tug, one that called me back yet pushed me away at the same time.

A tall shade tree, its leaves curling in advance of winter, overlooked our group as we knelt on the moist ground. Kenny led us in prayer and I looked away, over the top of the two gravestones, especially my mother's, where the inscription read, "I am the vine, you are the branches, says the Lord."

I listened to the soft, muted whistle of a Long Island Railroad train pass in the distance and I remembered how my mother had loved that gospel, the message that no branch could exist separate of the vine which nurtured it.

I had cut that vine, and I was cutting it still.

"So how you been?" Kenny said, as our group disbanded and we walked to our cars. Rosemary offered to take their three boys home in their Honda, while Kenny stayed behind and had a chance to catch up with me. I owed Kenny. He had given up a lot for me after our mother died, but this was payback time, I sensed.

"I'm sorry I missed your police ceremony with the Mayor this summer."

He motioned for me to toss him the keys to my car. "Hey, no problem. I'm sure you were busy with your work at the TV station in Chicago. How did that job work out anyway?"

I flipped him my keys. "I'm onto something new."

He got behind the wheel and we pulled onto Old Country Road and headed east to Hicksville, where Kenny and Rosemary lived in the house where Kenny and I had grown up.

"I heard you met Clinton," he said, his eyes focused straight ahead as he drove. Kenny was like our dad, solid. That summer he had broken down the door of a crack house in Brooklyn after a call had come in about a rape. None of the bullets fired by the three crackheads hit him, though they parted what was left of his hair, and the Mayor of New York gave him the City's highest medal for bravery.

"Yeah, I met Clinton. I doubt he aced his class in Compromise 101."

"In the ballpark where he plays you do it right the first time, or you're dead. No second chances."

I shifted gears on the conversation. "How're the cops treating you?"

"Fine. But I broke the cardinal rule."

"What's that?"

"Don't outshine the brass. The Captain didn't like all the press I got, and they reassigned me to a new trouble spot in the city."

"Dangerous?"

"They're all dangerous, but yeah, this one is especially hot."

"What does Rosemary say about that?"

"She doesn't know how intense it is, but I got another job lined up. Something that can be my substitute if I choose to retire from the cops."

"That's good, especially if the new assignment is dangerous."

"I wanted to talk to you about it before I talk to Rosemary, though, and make my decision. But you never answered the letter I sent you."

"I've been really busy," I said as we pulled up to the house. His boys' faces appeared in the living room window, their noses flattened against the glass as they waved to their dad.

"I got a chance to start a security company in the neighborhood," he said.

"Ah, no, Kenny. I hope this isn't about me."

"Actually I *was* thinking about you, the two of us, brothers. Working together."

"That's good for you, Kenny. But that's not my thing."

"We can cover all the way from Merrick to Farmingdale. We'll clear a hundred grand each. Take this opportunity with me, Colin, and I'll leave the police. That will make Rosemary happy."

The front door opened, and Rosemary, a pear-shaped curly-haired girl he had married while still in the police academy, stepped onto the stoop. She waved for us to come in. "Dinner's ready."

"I can't, Kenny, really. I got a job already."

"A job?"

"Yeah, in Boston, with a television station."

"I can't believe you. You would turn down family?"

"Kenny?" Rosemary called from the stoop as we continued to sit in the car. "Dinner."

"A big-time TV reporter. She hired me this week. She said she needs me."

"I can't believe it. You couldn't save Mom, so now you're gonna save distressed women."

"I didn't say she was distressed. I said she needed me."

He stepped out of the car as his three boys ran to him and hugged his legs. "Look, you do what you want, OK," he said, and he walked toward the house.

"Kenny!" I called, as he climbed up the front steps. "It's my life, right?"

He turned to me. "That girl, the one who hired you. Is she the one Clinton told me about?"

"I don't know, what did Clinton tell you?"

"'She eats nails,' he said."

"Screw you, Kenny."

"What was that about?" Rosemary said, whispering, but he waved her off as he stepped into the house. Inside, Kenny was quiet as Rosemary set the table. I played "Go Fish" with his boys until Rosemary called Kenny and me to the table before the pot roast got cold.

"I'm sorry, Colin," he said, without looking at me.

"Potatoes?" Rosemary said.

"I'm sorry I put that knock on your girl," Kenny said, as he scooped potatoes with a spoon.

Rosemary ladled string beans onto his plate, then signaled toward his lap. "Kenneth. Your napkin."

Still, I didn't answer, and I smoothed my napkin before Rosemary could remind me.

"It's OK," I said, but I didn't look at him, and the only sound during dinner was the clinking of silverware.

Back at the station, my first encounter with Junior went well.

"Who hired you?" was his opening line.

"Nice to see you, too, Junior," I said, as the morning team gathered in the Channel 6 newsroom his first day on the job after transferring to Boston from Philadelphia.

"My name is Steven."

"Is that with a 'ph' or a 'v?' Or should I just cut to 'asshole?'"

Bridget stepped in. "I hired him, Steven. That was my call."

"We're cutting staff, not adding staff, Maloney."

"I've added Colin Patrick to my team, and you can see me about that if you have any problem, OK?"

That shut him up, but he glared at me as he turned in his chair and returned to his computer.

Stan, ever the mediator, stepped in, "Well, good morning, everyone. We have a big agenda on the Runner in Red docket today. Mr. Freddie Norman, a special guest, will be joining us on Heartbreak Hill. Let's all saddle up and make our way over there for Mr. Norman's presentation, shall we?"

We went in two cars, Stan, Bridget and me in one, and Junior in another. We turned off Route 16 and onto Commonwealth Ave., where Stan and I had walked earlier. He parked just short of Centre Street.

"This is it, I believe, the tree in question," Stan said, and he tapped a tall strapping oak. "Colin, will you get some video of this? Get shots of this tree in the can for later use."

I didn't know the purpose, but I shot the tree from different angles when a third car pulled up and Roman got out, along with a tiny white-haired man.

"Morning, Mr. Roman," Stan said, but Roman ignored him and walked directly over to Bridget. He was tall, tanned and imperially thin with slick black hair, but stiff, too, the kind of guy who stood so straight it looked like he still had his coat hanger in his jacket. He was all smiles with his slick coif as he approached Bridget but she gave him a perfunctory nod.

Stan introduced me. "Mr. Roman, this is Colin, Bridget's new cameraman. He worked for you in Philadelphia where folks I talked to said good things about his work."

"That's why we pay people," Roman said, flatly, without looking at me and he gave another smile in Bridget's direction. Still, she didn't bite. Then he turned to the tiny white-haired man.

"Group, this is Freddie Norman, from Toronto, Canada. Let's get right to it, OK? Freddie, why don't you show everyone the photograph you brought and tell us your story."

"Yessir, I'm Freddie Norman, from Toronto. I've lived there my whole life, my 71 years. Been a runner my whole life, too. Ran

76 marathons in my time, including seven Boston Marathons from 1950 to 1959."

"Show them your photograph," said Junior.

"Yessir, this here photo is a picture of a tree, this here tree," he said, and he pointed to the tall oak I had just photographed. "The tree is bigger now, of course, since it's growed a lot since 1951. But this is the tree I was running by when I saw her, the girl in the red hood."

"Excuse me," Stan said. "You saw a girl in a red hood in 1951."

"Yessir. Right here, in this spot. In front of this here tree, and the girl is in the picture, as you can see. My wife took the picture. That's not Tim Finn in the picture. I ran against Tim Finn every race I did in Boston, from 1950 to 1959, and this is a picture of a runner in a red hood who is girl-shaped. Tim Finn was not girl-shaped then and never will be girl-shaped."

He passed the photo around and Bridget studied it intently before looking over at Roman, who smiled broadly now—a *gotcha* smile. Still, Bridget shook her head.

"I don't know," she said. "This could be a woman, or it could be a teenage boy. I can't say for sure." Then she turned to Freddie Norman. "Did you talk to the runner in this picture?"

"No, but I heard Tim Finn talk to her. He was in front of us, out of the picture, and I heard him call to her. 'Stay up, Delaney,' he shouted over his shoulder. 'You can do it, stay up.'"

"Tim Finn used the name, 'Delaney?' You say he called back over his shoulder to talk to this runner in the red hood?'"

"Yes ma'am, he called her Delaney. I say 'her' because she was girl-shaped. And Tim Finn ain't girl-shaped. Never was.'"

"Did you tell this news to Pop Gallagher?"

"Of course I did. I went up to him at the finish line. But you know Pop. Everyone knows how pig-headed Pop was then and I'm sure he is still. He insisted the runner in the red hood was Tim Finn, because Tim had a red hood, too, and the reporters believed Pop that Tim was the only one that day with a red hood. I didn't have this picture of course. Not till last month after my wife saw Mr. Roman's ad in the newspaper up our way in Toronto asking if anyone had pictures from the 1951 Boston Marathon. My wife went through old boxes to find this picture. Of course reporters back then wrote in their stories that it was Tim Finn in the red hood, since that's what Pop told them. Everyone believed Pop and nobody believed me."

"Thank you, Freddie," Roman said, and he gestured for Junior to take the old man back to the station, while signaling that he wanted to stay a moment and talk to Bridget. Freddie hesitated, saying, "Now, hold on a minute, Mr. Roman. Pop made it like I lied, when really it was Pop who was not telling the truth. I don't want people to think I'm a liar."

"Right, right, whatever," Roman said, gesturing again to Junior who leaned in close to the old man as he led him away and said, "You can relax, nobody's going to doubt you anymore."

Bridget was responsive to Roman suddenly, even as he stepped in closer to her. This time she didn't push back.

"If this is true, Bridget," Stan said. "It means Pop was either careless about the truth, or was actively working to cover up the truth. Not good for him either way, since he was the guardian of the rules."

"But good news for you, Bridget," said Roman. "This gives you the leverage you need. Once you find this woman—the Runner in Red—you'll be in a position to destroy Pop."

"I'm not eager to destroy him. I just want him to stop training my daughter."

"Whatever," Roman said. "You've got a name now, 'Delaney.' I'll have my team in New York scour City Hall in Boston and go through the archives. We'll find Delaney.'"

He motioned to Stan and me to step away so he could talk to Bridget alone. We did, but I could hear him in my earpiece as he took Bridget by the hand and walked her to a grassy patch twenty yards away, and I realized Bridget was wearing a live mic.

"You're the bright light in the family, Bridget," I could hear Roman say. "Jack tags along, always has. Why not use this opportunity to come back to me?"

"He's my husband."

"I read in the *Herald* that you threw him out of the house."

"Howie Carr exaggerates. I never tossed his clothes out the bedroom window in the rain."

"My sources say you've been having trouble with Jack a long time, not just the estranged part since Ellen got hit by the car in Oregon, but things have gotten worse since Pop began training Ellen again."

"Love means you can look someone in the eye, even if you're estranged, and like what you see, Steve. I stopped being able to do that with you in 1971."

"I hear Jack's a bit out of sorts, now that you've started seeing me again. That doesn't have to be a bad thing, Bridget."

"I'm seeing you, Steve. But I'm not *seeing* you. Let's keep our terms straight, OK."

"Still, how long can you keep going home to dinner-for-one?"

"Longer than it would be worth your while to wait. But I thank you for the assignment. We'll make this happen."

She turned and walked away, signaling to Stan and me to return to our car. But as we walked, she said to me, "Did you hear that?"

And I realized she had worn the live mic on purpose.

CHAPTER SEVEN

Bridget went to New York to coordinate with Roman's team and devise a strategy to research more on "Delaney." While she was away Stan sent me to the library where I was fast becoming an expert on women's running.

Few women throughout history had ever tried to run a marathon, I learned as I read hundreds of newspaper accounts and watched tapes from the archives at Boston Public Library, my new home away from home.

One legend told of a woman, Melpomene, who slipped into the marathon in the 1896 Olympics in Athens. Over the next seventy years—before rules were changed to permit women to compete officially at distances greater than 200 meters—a handful of women "crashed" marathons, pressing for the right to run, including Marie Ledru in France in 1918, Violet Percy in 1926, Dale Greig in England in 1964, and Mildred Sampson in New Zealand in 1964. The Runner in Red, should it be proved—and a name identified—would be the first woman to have accomplished the feat on American soil.

As I watched videotapes of old Boston Marathons, working fourteen hour days to gather background before Bridget's return, I found one clip that showed Bill Rodgers stopping at the crest of Heartbreak Hill to take a sip of water during the 1975 Boston Marathon. Asked why he would stop while thousands of runners chased up the slope behind him, Rodgers, who won the 1975 race in record time, said, "If the pace is fast, it helps if I pause to catch my breath."

And so I pause also, not simply to catch my breath, but to take a break from the narrative at this point and provide product of the research I collected. When the pace is fast—as Bill Rodgers said—it's useful to lay out the background, in this case, the important contributions made to the running game by the early women runners, the "women pioneers of Boston," as Stan called them.

Bridget was in high school during the mid-1960s when, on a cool April day in 1966, 24-year-old Roberta Gibb jumped out from behind a bush at the start of the Boston Marathon. She had applied for admission to the race, but Jock Semple, who worked as a trainer at Boston Garden and assigned the marathon numbers in between his duties as a trainer for the Boston Bruins, had scratched, "Reject," on her application and sent it back.

Not to be deterred, Gibb had ridden a bus into town from the west coast and tucked in with the crowd in Hopkinton that gray day in 1966, and the men, sympathetic, shielded her from the view of the officials' truck. Dressed in a bulky sweatshirt with a one-piece black bathing suit underneath, Gibb forged ahead, worried she might be spotted, but she was not, and she completed the entire distance in 3:21:40, thus becoming (aside from the 'Runner in Red' possibility) the first woman to run the Boston Marathon.

The next year, 1967, Jock assigned Kathrine Switzer a number by mistake after the Syracuse coed mailed in her application, using her initials, "K.V. Switzer."

Jock missed it, but Pop spotted the mistake the next morning when he stopped in at the Garden following his night-shift at the airport working on a cargo loading dock, his full-time job. It was his practice to check on Jock to make sure his co-director partner was doing his job assigning marathon numbers competently, but Jock did not appreciate the special attention from his former running rival.

"Blast it, mon," Jock roared in his Scottish burr after Pop advised Jock to call the applicant and ask for the full name as rules required. "He's a Kevin or Karl, mon, let it go. We'll never see the imbecile again anyway."

The day of the race, however, the sportswriters spotted the error. "Hey, guys, you got a broad in your race," they shouted two miles after the start. "And she's wearing one of your official numbers."

With that, Pop and Jock were off the bus—reprising their competitive fire from days past—as they tried to beat each other down the road to retrieve the number and restore the sanctity of the Boston Marathon's rules.

As all the world knows, thanks to the UPI photographer positioned perfectly for the shot, Jock beat Pop that day and the three photos depicting the action —Jock chasing K. V. Switzer, Jock reaching in to rip the number, 261, off her sweatshirt, and finally, K. V. Switzer's huge boyfriend leaning his shoulder into Jock to propel Jock toward a ditch—ran Page One around the world and effectively helped launch the campaign to open the marathon to women.

What Johnny Carson couldn't do by poking fun at Jock, four years later, Bridget's "Stand-off at the Finish line" with Pop in the 1971 race served as the coup de grace, and the next year, 1972, the Boston Marathon officially opened the race to women.

Nina Kuscsik of New York won the first formal women's division in 1972 in a time of 3:10:36. By that point, following her incident with Pop the year before, Bridget had given up running, which I learned from patching together accounts from several magazines.

She broke up with her boyfriend, Steve Roman, and moved to San Francisco where she kept a low profile. Roman and Jack Maloney, the other runner she had shared stardom with in college, moved to Martha's Vineyard to paint houses while they trained for the 1972 Olympics. Then fate interceded as one day Jack Maloney left his ice tea on a porch in the hot sun. When he climbed down from his ladder for a sip the drink had warmed and he put cool strawberries in the glass. "Hmmmm," he said, and he bid Roman to come down off his ladder to have a taste.

The next day they made a bigger jug of the stuff and invited the other house painters to try it. Soon Jack Maloney, who possessed a silver tongue, convinced a local bottler to let them use his facility at night to bottle their concoction. While Roman applied for a trademark, Jack hiked all over the Vineyard convincing store owners to carry their drink, called "Runner's Delight."

The beverage took off and without knowing it Jack Maloney and Steve Roman had created Snapple before Snapple.

They sold their trademark to Pepsi, who paid them one hundred thousand dollars for the rights, but Jack and Roman fell out after Roman, who insisted he had created the greater value by engineering the trademarking process, signed up the rights 90/10 his way. Jack, who never paid attention to fine details, got snookered, while Roman trucked to Wall Street with his take and grew that during Wall Street's go-go days of the 80s into a small fortune.

By this point Jack had moved to Boston and had turned his gift for gab into an insurance job, but most significantly, one night he climbed in his car and set out for San Francisco to scour the city looking for Bridget. Finding her down and out, he convinced her to come home and marry him, and by the mid-70s, while Roman was starting to build his empire in New York, Bridget was back in Boston with Jack, as his wife, and a young mother.

I hit a barren patch and couldn't find out any more information on the family until I came across an issue of *Runner's World* from that spring, with a story titled, "Comeback Gal?"

It told how Ellen Crutchfield, who under an intense training regimen tailored to her by her grandfather, Pop Gallagher, was fast regaining her world-class form after her failure at the Olympic Trials and a car accident in Oregon. She was making strong progress, but according to the author, she needed a major victory to convince the skeptics that the once rising star could be a national champion again.

The story filled in some blanks for me: as a ninteteen-year-old college freshman on coach Randy Thomas's team at Boston College, Ellen had run the Philadelphia Marathon in 2:32:14, and had set an American junior's record. That had prompted her in her sophomore year to want to become the youngest Olympic champion ever and she trained hard with Pop, a former trainer of champions, which created a rift between mother and daughter.

Ellen led the Olympic Trials for twenty miles that spring of her sophomore year at BC, but she developed a stress fracture and though she finished the race, she hobbled across the line in 10th place and in frustration at the "told you so's" from her mother, she quit running, dropped out of school and married a classmate.

The marriage didn't work out, and two years later she moved to Oregon, to try for a comeback with Nike. But she failed to make the team, and one evening while running alone she was hit by a car on a desolate stretch of country road outside Eugene and lay in a ditch overnight until hunters discovered her the next morning. During a slow and painful recovery her grandfather penciled her a note from Boston.

"The champion you are is waiting inside you," he wrote. "Come home and we will put wind in your sails and send your ships to sea."

She was in her mid-20's by this point and she moved back to Boston. She moved in with her father into the house he had kept after he and Bridget had separated three years earlier. Her father, Jack Maloney, gave full endorsement to her training with Pop again, the story said, and this did not sit well with Bridget who by that point was working for a television station in Philadelphia.

"Admittedly, things are strained with my mom and me after my choice to train for a comeback with my grandfather," Ellen said. "But I will beat the demons."

She responded under Pop's nurturing eye, and she ran sub 33 minutes for the 10K three times that spring. Despite the continuing tug between Pop and her mother, and the emotional tax involved with that, she set an American record for the half marathon in June, which was the basis for the article.

"She won't have the credentials to be a favorite at New York this November," which was now a month away, the story said. "But this 'Comeback Gal' could surprise!"

I drove to Pop's house to see Ellen—eager to try to see if I could patch things up with her—but no one answered. I tried again the next morning, but still I got no response when I rang the bell. I left a note, "Call me," but no call came that night, or the next day, so I drove back to knock on the door again.

"You casing the place?" said a kid on a bike who eyed me.

"What?" I said as I returned to my car at the curb.

"I seen you watching the house when I went to school yesterday. Then again this morning I seen you. In the movies that's how guys case a place."

"I'm looking for the girl who moved in here with her grandfather."

"Oh, you want the road runner."

"Yeah. The road runner."

"Nice looking chick, though she's too skinny for my tastes." The kid was maybe 10.

"You have any idea where I might find her?"

"Try the track at Hyde Park High. That's where the old dude coaches high school runners."

I thanked him, but he held out his palm. "Like in the movies," he said. "They pay for information."

I gave him a five.

"Ooh, big spender," he said, and off he pedaled on his Huffy as I headed for Hyde Park High three miles away.

The sun set through a mask of gray clouds on a spring-like October afternoon as I approached the athletic field at Hyde Park High School. A group of boys in sweat suits walked for the gate following their workout, while behind them in the distance, Ellen wore a yellow singlet and shorts. She strode powerfully around the cinder track as Pop, wearing his gray jacket and peak cap, barked orders.

"Faster, lass," he shouted. "Stay strong, you'll last long."

His bark carried across the field as I passed the boys. "Man, she's awesome," said one, while another added, "She'll be kickin' some Ruskie and Kenyan butt in New York next month, that's for sure."

I stood at the gate watching Ellen run, impressed by her long, powerful stride, her erect shoulders, the smooth churning of her legs and the easy swinging of her arms—and of course, her blonde ponytail flapping.

"What the hell you doin'?" Pop shouted, as I walked to the top of the turn for a closer look and he swung his arms at me as if shooing the cat. "Get away!"

"It's all right, Pop," Ellen said, as she interrupted her run and trotted over.

"What the hell you doin'?" Pop shouted at me, his thick white eyebrows arched like a tiger's back. "Upsetting the girl's workout!"

"He's OK, Pop," she said, stepping between us to save me from destruction.

"I am?"

"Who told you I was here?"

"Let's say I stumbled upon you."

"Come on, Ellen," Pop said. "I want you running, I don't want you talking."

She turned to me. "I'm not ready."

"I just want to talk to you."

"I'm not ready for a relationship, and that includes talking," she said, and she jogged away as Pop ambled back to his spot in the middle of the straightaway, hot as an iron still. But as Ellen passed me at the top of the turn on her next lap, I shouted, "Your mother loves you."

This stopped her in her tracks. "What did you say?"

"I talked to your mother about you."

"When?" she said, as she sauntered over, hand on hip.

"I'm going to see her again when she gets back from New York. I'm sure we'll talk some more about you."

"She's in New York?"

"For two weeks."

Ellen turned away in disgust. "That damn Roman," she said, as the breeze played with her hair, wafting the loose golden strands that had come free from her ponytail during her hard run.

"Your mom said she loves you more than anyone can know."

"When can we talk?"

"Whenever you want."

"Thursday. The Ritz. You know where that is?"

"The Ritz? A hotel?"

"On Arlington Street. 3pm. Ask for Bailey at the front desk," she said, and she darted off. Pop marched toward me to yell again, but I preempted him by waving good-bye and he bought it.

He returned to his coaching spot in the middle of the track, but as Ellen passed me again on the turn, she shouted something.

"What?" I said, but I missed it, and I waited for her to come around again on another lap.

"Bring your running stuff," she said over her shoulder as she sprinted by me.

Then she was gone again, around the turn and down the straightaway, running hard, blonde ponytail pounding wildly across her shoulders as Pop hollered, "Stay strong, lass. You'll last long."

CHAPTER EIGHT

Junior assigned Bridget to do a feature on young girls buying track shoes at a downtown mall. She told him she was busy, but he reminded her who was boss.

"You'll find the shoe store in the Prudential Center Mall. The manager is waiting for you. Take your boy with you," he said, too self-absorbed to realize that the icy stare she gave him burned hotter than a sunspot.

The owner of the running store in the mall—a round man with Chia Pet hair, pink shirt, and a green cardigan—clapped when we walked in.

"Girls, girls, get ready," he said, as he turned to half a dozen giggling high school girls seated with boxes of "Women First" shoes on their laps.

Bridget, ever the pro, shook hands with each of the girls making them comfortable as I unpacked my camera and set up for a shot of the girls trying on the shoes, bouncing on their toes, smiling—most of all smiling, as the paper Junior gave Bridget specified. Behind us, a tiny man in his 60s with bright blue eyes, a mop of hair and a Bobby Kennedy profile walked in. Dressed in a faded windbreaker, he looked perplexed as if he had wandered into the wrong room. It was Bridget who saw him first.

"John?" she said. "Young John?"

"Jesus, Bridget Maloney. How are you doing, how's your dad?"

"Dad...oh, he's fine," she said, but the tiny man—realizing his mistake—apologized, as Bridget called me over to introduce me to Johnny Kelley, whose picture I had seen in countless news stories during my research.

Called "Young John," to distinguish him from John A. Kelley (the Elder), the champion from Pop's era, John J. Kelley (no relation, but called the Younger) had won the Boston Marathon in 1957. The star of Jock Semple's B.A.A. team, Young John had competed in two Olympics, in 1956 and '60, and was the American national marathon champion eight times in a row, a record yet to be broken.

"Young John is the link between the early runners and the champions of the 70s such as Bill Rodgers, Frank Shorter, Amby Burfoot and Jack Fultz, Bobby Hodge, Greg Meyer, Randy Thomas, Vinnie Fleming, Dickie Mahoney, so many others," Bridget said. "He was the premier runner of his era in the 50s and my inspiration."

"Don't let your dad hear you say nice things. I ran for Jock's B.A.A., remember."

"What are you doing here, John, I thought you lived in Connecticut? Still driving a cab?"

"I do and I am. But I gave my copy of Kerouac's *On the Road* to a friend and I stopped by to pick up a new copy. I know every pebble from Hopkinton to Boston, Bridget, but I can't find Barnes and Noble. I must be getting old."

"You'll always be young to me, John," she said, adding, "I've got a question, do you mind?"

"For you, Bridget, anything."

"What do you remember about the Runner in Red?"

"Not much. But Jock never believed Pop's version of the story."

"How do you mean?"

"Jock never believed that Tim Finn was the runner in the red hood that the Canadians said they saw that day. I think Jock always believed the Canadians were telling the truth."

"Really? Jock said that?"

"Not in so many words. He was livid that Pop's D.A.A. won the team prize because he thought Pop had pulled a fast one. Jock used to say the only way Pop's D.A.A. beat our B.A.A. boys was by putting a girl on his team."

"A girl? Jock believed Pop put a woman on the D.A.A. team?"

"Jock never accused Pop directly, but he did call Pop's victory a phony win. 'Tim Finn's Ringer' he used to say. 'Pop won in '51 because Tim Finn brought a ringer.'"

"Jock believed the D.A.A. team had a 'ringer,' a woman, on their team? Somebody fast enough to affect the final score?"

"You know Jock and your dad. They were always going back and forth at each other. One would blast one, then the other would blast the other. We never took it seriously when they got into name-calling. So the Runner in Red is still just an urban legend to me, Bridget."

She was silent a moment as she absorbed his words, then she motioned to John to step out onto the concourse so she could direct him to the bookstore. That's when I noticed a young boy at the back of the store slink behind a row of running jackets. He wore a Seattle Mariner's cap backward, and his eyes darted side to side as he watched the clerk at the cash register.

Chia didn't miss him though. "Hey," the owner shouted, as the kid shoved a pair of basketball shoes under his coat and bolted for the door. He would have been out of the store except for the obstacle presented by Bridget who was returning after saying goodbye to Young John.

Over they went, Bridget and the kid, and I rushed to lift her up as the store owner reached for the Mariner kid, by the neck.

"Thief!" he shouted. "Third time he robs me."

"Third time?" Bridget said, dusting herself off.

"What's with the schools? Where's our tax money go? Can't the schools keep these hoodlums inside during the day?"

"You say this boy stole from you three times."

"Damn right," said the owner who took out a notebook with

dates on it. "This is a story you should cover. What are the schools doing with our tax money?"

"I agree," Bridget said, and she wrote down the dates as a mall security guard, heavy on tattoos, arrived in a rush to take the kid away by the collar.

"Where we going?" I said to Bridget as she motioned to me to pack up my gear.

"We're blowin' off the puff piece."

I parked our van in the lot beside the athletic field at Hyde Park High School. Bridget got out and in her Ann Taylor best stormed across the field—the same field where I had watched Ellen practice. Boys and girls formed small groups on the track as Pop directed workouts for each group. Bridget came to a stop in front of his toes before Pop acknowledged her arrival.

"Where's Tim Finn?"

"Nearly thirty years you don't talk to me and that's all you can say, 'Where's Tim Finn?'"

"Let me be more specific—where's Tim Finn's Ringer?"

Pop's eyes burned beneath his peak cap. "Oh, now you're parroting Semple, are you?" He gathered the high school kids for the start of their workout. "We'll go with the boys first." Then he paused. "No, this time, let's go with the girls first."

I could see Bridget bristle as a dozen boys, all shapes and sizes, stepped back on the track to let a dozen girls in Hyde Park t-shirts toe the line ahead of them.

"If that's your bone to political correctness, you're thirty years late," said Bridget as Pop fired his starter's pistol and off the girls went on their first lap around the track.

"I tried to make peace with you. But you're filled with hate. Boys get ready," Pop said.

74

The boys stepped to the line and again Pop fired his pistol—off they went.

"And what are you filled with, love?"

"Yes, love for my race, that you took away."

"You created the situation yourself. But's that's always been your hallmark, your overarching pride."

"You bet I had pride. But you cared nothing for the rules."

"Your rules."

"No, the rules of the game. You never cared about rules, before it was fashionable to run."

"Fashionable? You think that's why I ran? I was taunted for wanting to run, for being a woman."

"I was pelted with snowballs in the 30s."

"At least nobody grabbed your ass!"

Incensed, Pop spun away. He crossed the track onto the infield where he could watch the boys and girls, the two groups, stride along the back straight-away.

Bridget followed him. "I'm not here to argue proprietorship of the Boston Marathon. I want to talk about Tim Finn."

In the distance, Tim Finn, wearing tan cargo pants and a faded jean jacket, came walking toward them. But his smile disappeared the instant he saw Bridget.

"Tell me, Tim. What do you remember about the 1951 Boston Marathon?" she asked as he arrived at Pop's side and handed him a clipboard.

"We won the team trophy."

"Do you remember Freddie Norman? He remembers you."

He was clearly upset by the questioning and he didn't meet her eye. "That was a long time ago, Bridget. All I remember is the day was a proud moment for America and for our D.A.A. team that made it possible."

Pop turned to face the group. He watched them complete their first lap and pass in front of him as he stood on the edge of the track.

"Way to go, girls, stay strong—you'll last long!"

Bridget's eyes reflected hurt as he offered the girls encouragement. When they had passed, she said, "You wouldn't let me cross the line. Why the great interest in my daughter to see she gets across the line first?"

"Ellen has a pure, natural talent."

"She's not related to you, either."

"It wasn't because you weren't related to me that I said what I did."

"Then why did you say it?"

"Because I knew it would stop you."

The look in her eyes showed the wound still cut deep as he drifted across the field to a place where he could stand alone. It was clear by his body language that he was finished with the conversation, and after a long moment, Bridget turned, and shaking her head, started back toward our van. I followed her, as did Tim Finn.

"Why didn't he do that for me, Tim?" she said, gesturing to the string of girls running on the track.

"Nobody did that for you, Bridget. You and your generation get credit for opening the way for these young girls today."

"Did you call out to a runner, 'Stay up, Delaney?' Did you run the Boston Marathon in '51 with somebody named Delaney, Tim? Freddie Norman says you did.'"

He flinched and it was obvious her words hit a mark. "I paid my debt, Bridget. Five years in the slammer. I paid my debt to society for my mistake. I wish I could help you, but I can't."

She nodded, signaling she was OK with that.

"I'm not a strong man, Bridget. I'm sorry."

"I'm going to have to talk to you again, you know that."

"I wish I could help you," was all he said as we arrived at the van. Then he turned and walked back to Pop.

When we were in the van and moving down the road I said, "What was that all about, five years in the slammer?"

"Tim worked for the City of Boston in the 1970s. His job was to oversee the Child Services Department. He approved an application for an adoption that went bad. A baby from Central America. The father in the adopting family in Boston abused the child and that flew back at Tim, since he had falsified the application to move it forward. He lost his job, it tanked his career, and he did five years in Walpole Prison. But he's a good man. He could have taken people at the Catholic adoption agency down with him, but he took full responsibility. He's loyal and he's always been good to me."

"How so?"

"He was one of four Finn brothers on Pop's D.A.A. team. He was second fastest to his brother, Joe, who's now the governor. They lived in the neighborhood. Tim taught me how to ride a bike and he would take me to fairs. He bought me ice cream and won dolls for me. I called him 'Uncle Tim.' He's a good man."

"What's he do now?"

"He takes care of Pop. His brother, Joe, the governor, has him on the state payroll as an administrative assistant—a gofer. But mostly he takes care of Pop, and he uses his own money to do that. Even Howie Carr, who spends his life impaling government gofers in his newspaper column, doesn't pick on Tim because everyone knows Tim's good people. There's something going on here with Pop, I can smell it. But Tim won't snitch. He's loyal."

I thought of Tim Finn as the guy who had put a shoulder into my chest and moved me out the door at Pop's house. But if Bridget was willing to give him a pass, so was I.

Fraudulent adoptions. Walpole Prison. Gofer jobs.

I was new to all this, the running game, but I was developing a deeper and richer understanding of how life worked in Dorchester.

CHAPTER NINE

met another member of Pop's D.A.A. team, Bailey, when I went to the front desk at the Ritz. A muffin of a man in his 60s, he was dressed in a starched Ritz uniform. He gave me Ellen's room number, 721, and told me to go up. "Miss Maloney is waiting for you."

I knocked, tentatively, but when Ellen opened the door, dressed in black acrylic tights and red top, she smiled. "You found it, I see."

"Who's Bailey, and what's going on?"

"Bailey works the front desk. He used to run for Pop's Dorchester team. When I run the river he lets me change here."

"In a Ritz Carlton suite?"

"He loves Pop. Did you bring your running stuff?"

"Yeah," I said, as I lifted my paper bag and she pointed to the bathroom where I could get changed.

"I see you go for designer carrying cases."

"You're not going to blow me away out there, are you?"

"You'll probably push me to a new world record."

"Where we going?"

"Get dressed. We're running the Charles today."

As I got dressed in the bathroom I wondered if my ankle would make it, but after everything I had done to get this far I would have hopped along the Charles to be with Ellen.

"Bailey said, 'Maloney.' What happened to 'Crutchfield?'" I said through the bathroom door.

"My divorce came through this week, finally."

"Wow, long time. What, three years?"

"He didn't make it easy."

"That bad, huh?" I said, as I stepped out of the bathroom.

She looked at my bulky gray sweats and basketball shoes. "You're not a runner are you?"

"I guess I do look like Rocky Balboa."

"Yes, that bad," she said. "But the nightmare is over, finally. Ready to run?"

"Ready," I said, and I didn't ask for details, though I was dying to know.

We crossed Commonwealth Avenue, and at Beacon Street crossed the Arthur Fiedler footbridge to the Esplanade. Then we turned left and picked up the macadam running path along the river. Trees, gold and red with autumn, swayed overhead as she strode smoothly and I puffed along beside her under a blue October sky, my ankle A-OK, and I savored the moment, never dreaming I could have come this far in such a short time with her.

"You run well," she said, being kind. I told her about the Red Sox and she shot me a pained look. "I'm sorry."

"Way it goes," I said.

Traffic from Storrow Drive zipped to our left. On the right, the river wore diamonds as the afternoon sun slanted in the west and created sparkles. We ran past mothers with strollers, and lovers holding hands.

"Can I ask you about something?" I said.

"Of course."

"Why is Pop training you?"

"Oh, right out of the starting blocks and into the big questions, I see."

"I thought he was the enemy of women runners."

Twenty, thirty yards passed and she said, "People change."

"Pop changed?"

"I think he's always been different with me."

"Really?"

"Can I tell you a story?" She didn't wait for my answer. "When I was small I loved to stay with Pop and my grandmother. I loved going with him to his neighborhood races in Hyde Park, Jamaica Plain, wherever. He wasn't with the Boston Marathon then. That was after he quit. After they dropped him."

"Seems to me he earned his ticket out of town," I said, my tone sharper than I intended.

"That's my mother talking."

"You think Pop was justified to block her?"

"She hurt him."

"Oh?"

"On Sunday afternoons after he had wrapped up his neighborhood races he would take me to Castle Island in South Boston. He always loved to walk around Castle Island, to be close to the sea. He missed the sea, he said, from his boyhood in Ireland. He said the sea made him sad, but the sea excited him too and he would point to the ships sailing out of the channel into Boston Harbor, heading for the open waters. He would tell me the big broad world out there could be mine.

"'Lassie, someday we're going to send your ships out to the open sea,' he would tell me. I learned to dream big dreams from Pop.'"

"He was never that way with your mother."

"She hurt him."

"How?

"I don't know, but one time as we walked along the beach he stared at the water. 'Your mother has given me great pain,' he said.'"

"So he was mad at her before 1971?"

"Yes, obviously."

"Don't you think she has a right to be mad at him?" I said, and she looked at me, then looked away.

"I'm not exactly objective when it comes to my mother these days."

We ran silently for a stretch, the path passing below us as I stared into the distance, thinking. I was thinking about her mother, thinking how mad I would be if someone blocked me as I was about to set a world record, but when I glanced at Ellen again, she looked very sad.

"I'm sorry if I upset you."

"No. It's just my mom is strong. She fought hard so I could have all this. She and the other women who fought to get the rules changed."

"They fought Pop."

"Yes, they did."

"And he fought them."

"Yes, but my mother won't let go of it. She's made it her mission to get back at him, to keep hurting him. She'll never give up till she can hurt him every single day."

I didn't say anything, neither of us spoke, until I said, "You have a lot of feeling for both of them, don't you?"

"I love my mother, but I owe Pop a lot."

"Because of Castle Island?"

"No, because he saved me. In Oregon, after I got hurt."

"Tell me."

"My marriage had gone bust, and I moved out to Oregon to try for a comeback with Nike. But that went bust, too. One day I got hit by a car and I thought I'd never see the light again. That's when Pop reached out to me. He gave me the encouragement to pick myself up. The ships sailing for the open sea, that kind of thing. He encouraged me to come back to Boston and he offered to help me make a comeback. He continues to encourage me, every day. And that has put me in a difficult spot with my mom. That's why this is so important to me, to win Boston. I want to do it for Pop. He never won Boston. I want to give him something back for everything he's done for me."

"You think your mother is interested only in settling a grudge?"

"I do. She'll destroy herself. She will have obliterated me, my dad, everyone who means anything to her. For what? So she can say she found the Runner in Red.

"Your mother never told you about her finish line encounter with Pop, what he said to her to that day?"

"No, what did he tell her?"

"I should let her tell you that. That's not for me to say."

She looked at me as we followed the path below the BU Bridge. "All I know is that she is on a long spiral down. Why else would she let Roman use her? Roman knows she wants to embarrass Pop, and he'll give her whatever she wants. He still wants her, despite the bad blood and the way she dumped him in college."

I changed the subject. "Pop could take the first step. He could apologize to your mother."

"No. Pop and my mom are the same."

"How so?"

"Neither knows how to say they're sorry."

I looked at her, puzzled, "What does that mean?"

"Nobody can understand it, it's just old Irish."

We came to a sign that said "Cambridge," and she pointed to a bridge that crossed the Charles at River Street. "Let's turn around here."

We crossed the bridge and ran along Memorial Drive on the other side of the river in silence, until she said, "Maybe you can help."

"I don't know what I could do, really."

"She listens to you. You could talk sense to her."

"Listens to me? I don't think so."

"You're all I've got," she said, and I saw she was looking at me, into my eyes as we ran. We crossed the bridge at Mass. Ave. and began the final leg of our run back to the hotel, when suddenly she reached out to touch my hand, and I lit up warmly.

I rose as quickly as I did in baseball because I could hit the curve. I could previsualize the spot in the strike zone where the ball would dip as it zipped across the plate, and while other hitters might be fooled, I anticipated the break. "Stay back, stay back," I had taught myself well, and I waited on the curveball and hit it hard into the gap for an opposite-field double.

I could see the spin on the ball here, the pitch Ellen was throwing me, and I knew I had a choice to make: if I was going to have a chance with Ellen I was going to have to get involved. That meant stepping into the middle between her and her mom, a place I had avoided all my life, the confrontation zone, a place of ultimate vulnerability.

We returned to her room, and she closed the bathroom door. She turned the water on in the shower and I used the opportunity to sit in the big stuffed Ritz Carlton leather chair beside a tall window.

I listened to the pinging spray of the shower beyond the door and I recalled a line my father had recited when I was a boy and family crammed our tiny yard in Hicksville with Rheingold and ribs on warm summer days. "I wonder what the lonely people are doing today," my dad would say.

I smiled, thinking of my dad as the sun warmed my face, the muted horns of cars played below on Arlington Street, and the spray of the shower splintered off Ellen's golden body beyond the paneled door.

"Well?" she said, calling through the door and the sound of water. "Will you?"

I knew what she meant.

I closed my eyes against my reluctance to get entangled that went back not just ten years but all the way back, and I savored the moment—her interest in me—and I sank deep in my chair as I pondered my choice: I might be getting into the middle of something dangerous, getting in deeper by the minute, but damn it, I wasn't lonely anymore.

"For you, I'll do anything," I said.

The next morning I was shaving in my apartment when my cell rang. It was Bridget.

"Come to the window," she said. When I looked down I saw her in her car at the curb, motor running. "Get dressed, sweetie, you're not on banker's hours."

As we drove south on Dorchester Avenue through knots of traffic I asked her where we were going.

"Pop's house," she said. "Young John said Jock believed Pop had a girl on his team in 1951. I want to take a look."

"You never told Ellen what Pop said to you at the finish line in '71, did you? Does she know you're adopted?"

"Yes, she does."

"But she doesn't know the circumstances about how you learned, does she?"

"Nobody knows, Colin. I never told anyone, other than you."

"Any chance we could drop this whole thing?' I was taking a wild chance, hoping against hope, but I was not surprised by her response.

"No way!"

When we got to the front door of Pop's house Bridget took out a key and opened the door.

"You have a key?" I said.

"I lived here, sweetie, till college."

"Aren't you worried about barging in like this, that you might surprise him?"

"Pop goes to Mass every morning at this hour. That's a habit he learned from my mom, Mrs. Gallagher, and if there's one thing about Pop, he's habit-bound."

"What about Ellen? She's been staying here."

"I got a note from Jack, she's with him this week helping him with his books at his office in Waltham."

I followed her through the dark anteroom to the stairs and she knew right where she was going. At the top of the stairs there was a small room, an office, that had served as Pop's "Boston Marathon headquarters" for more than twenty years from the late 40s till Pop was released from his duties following his altercation with Bridget in 1971. It was a room she said she had been forbidden to enter while growing up, but now she made a beeline.

The room was filled with trophies, including the tall skyscraper size trophy from 1951 when Pop's D.A.A. won the team prize. Pictures of races from the 30s and 40s lined the walls, including heated contests between Pop and his arch running rival, Jock Semple, during the old days when both were young. Medals, dozens upon dozens of them, crammed the shelves of bookcases. As I perused the medals, Bridget opened the lid on a pink box. She smiled, as she picked through a series of frilly young girl's dresses.

"Ah, look at these, I haven't seen these in a lifetime!"

She told me how her mom, Mrs. Gallagher, had made them. "My mom, Pop's wife, was such a sweet woman. She was from Ireland and didn't say much. But she would take in laundry so she could afford to buy fabric to make me dresses, pink like this with bows. Every Saturday we would visit her sister in South Boston so she could show me off."

"Where was Pop?"

"He would drive us, but he never came into the house. He would sit outside in his car and do calculations for his road race the next day, in whatever town the race would be—Lynn, West Roxbury, Arlington— all over town. He lived for his D.A.A. boys and those Sunday road races."

Next, she opened a large oak box with a heavy top.

"This is Pop's treasure chest. This is where he keeps his most valuable items."

She sifted through the contents, handing them to me to inspect as well—including more photos from Pop's running days along with photos of the D.A.A. runners from the 50s pounding out victories on the roads.

"Whoa!" she said suddenly. "What's this doing here?"

She stood up straight as she examined a photo of three young nuns. They were smiling as they stood arm in arm in a garden. The photo said Kodak and had serrated edges. The date was March, 1959.

"This is a picture of Sister Josephine with two other nuns. I wonder what this is doing here, in Pop's treasure chest?"

I shrugged, but she said, "I better send this down to Roman in New York, see what his team can come up with."

Late Saturday afternoon that week, I called Ellen and asked if I could take her for a walk through downtown. She had said she wanted to go slow with relationships, but I chose to push the pace.

She agreed to come and I took her hand as we walked through the Public Garden and the Common under a crisp, blue October sky.

"You ever hear your mom talk about a Sister Josephine?" I said.

"No, who's that?"

"I was just wondering," I said and I dropped it.

We came to Fanueil Hall and passed the Bill Rodgers running store. She asked if we could go in. "My obsession with shoes," she said. "I can't help myself, I have to see what's new."

Charlie Rodgers, Bill's brother the store manager, recognized her and had her sit down so he could pull out samples of shoes that had come in since she'd been in the store last time, which from their banter back and forth indicated the interval had not been too long. Charlie was a warm, congenial guy with a handlebar moustache and he piled dozens of boxes in his arms.

"How about these?" he said, opening a box of "Women First."

"God, no," she said. "They stink!"

All three of us laughed, and what seemed like a hundred fittings later, Ellen and I were back out walking through the marketplace when we passed a Boston sports memorabilia kiosk. Ellen stopped when she spotted a baseball card, a shot of a guy—me—with a bat on his shoulder.

"Hey, look what we have here! This is somebody's rookie card."

"Yes, it is," I said, and I positioned myself in front of her with an imaginary bat on my shoulder. I struck a pose as if waiting for a pitch. "Stay back, stay back, that's how the good hitters do it. Stay back, wait as long as you can to see the pitch as best as you can, then you turn on it." I swung, smooth as can be, and laced the imaginary pitch deep into an upper deck.

"Stay back, huh?"

"That's baseball talk. But I don't want to do that in life anymore. I don't want to do that with you."

She smiled sheepishly and tapped the card. "They want three bucks for this."

"You won't break the bank."

"I'll keep it, see if it goes up in value," she said, and she bought the card.

Late Monday afternoon I was at the station when I got a call from Bridget. She was in New York and she wanted me to get my butt down to Manhattan as fast as I could. Obviously the photo of Sister Josephine had been significant.

"Roman's got big news for us," she said, and she gave me the name of the hotel where she was staying, the Waldorf, in room 890. "Fly down tonight. I've already booked you a room on my floor."

When I arrived at the Waldorf about midnight, I knocked on the door to Room 890 and Roman answered. He was in his pajamas, and none too pleased. He closed the door. *Slam!*

I was taken aback that Roman was in Bridget's room, and I turned a few circles trying to think what to do next, when I saw Bridget in her bathrobe come through the door at the end of the hallway. She was carrying a bucket of ice and had a big smile as she walked toward me.

"Roman's in your room," I said.

"I know," she said, matter of fact.

"You really think that's a good idea?"

"Why not?" she said, and she took a key from her bathrobe and opened the door to Room 896.

"What's this?" I said.

"My room."

"I thought you said…"

She got my drift and smiled very wide, amused. "I gave Roman my room, and I took this one. You're down the hall a bit further, Room 899."

"Then you're not in bed with him, so to speak?"

Another big smile. "You're my cameraman, Colin, you don't have to be my babysitter. See you bright and early at Roman's office on Park Ave. and 53rd."

CHAPTER TEN

The cell phone rang on the nightstand in my hotel room, waking me up in the dark.

"Colin, I need you to warn my mom."

"Huh, what?" I glanced at the clock on the nightstand. It was 5 am.

"My Dad went to New York to punch out Roman. My Dad's a hotheaded Irishman, Colin. I need you to warn my mom so she can stop him before he gets into trouble."

I tried calling Bridget at 7 am when I got up to get ready for our meeting with Roman at his office, but got no answer. I tried again before leaving for the meeting, but again got no answer so I went straight over to Park Ave and 53rd.

Roman's office was on the 50th floor. The lobby looked south offering a breathtaking view of lower Manhattan on a bright blue day. Bridget had not arrived and the receptionist had me sit in a waiting area in front of the main desk. I sat down beside a genial looking guy, tall with sandy hair, chiseled features, and a broad smile.

"Hi, you here to see the Robber Baron in Short Pants?"

"I'm waiting for Bridget Maloney."

"Me, too. Hi, I'm Jack Maloney," he said, and he extended his hand, with a firm grip.

Just then Bridget walked in, and Jack stood. He walked to her, as comfortable as if welcoming a guest into his own living room. "Hello, honey."

"Jack," said Bridget. "What are you doing here?"

"I came to look in on my old running partner," he said, adding, "Well, now that the gang's all here, shall we go in?"

He walked to the tall paneled doors that led to Roman's office and opened the door, making a long arching sweep with his arm to usher Bridget and me in ahead of him.

"Hello, asshole," he said to Roman, who sat behind a teak desk with an expansive view of the city behind him. An associate stood behind the desk at Roman's side looking over some papers with him. Roman looked up at us, but he did not smile.

"Too bad you didn't apply this same intensity to your running thirty years ago, Jack, you might have helped the team."

"I got the girl on the team, didn't I?"

"Then lost her."

"Now, guys!" Bridget said, but Roman didn't miss a beat. He stood at his chair and directed everyone to seats around his desk.

"Nice to have you join us, Jack, truly. You can see some work we've been doing to help your estranged wife advance her news career. Make yourself comfortable everyone, please. This is my research man, Steele. Usually I save Steele for bigger projects, but he has produced some interesting findings regarding the photo Bridget sent us."

Steele was a humorless guy, scrawny with slicked brown hair and designer glasses he wore, I'm sure, to upgrade his image. Roman passed out copies of the photo of the three nuns Bridget had found in Pop's chest.

"Go ahead, Steele," Roman said, "Share your news."

"We discovered that the photo is a picture of Delia Delaney standing with her sister, Sister Josephine."

"What?" Bridget said.

"Both Delia and Josephine were nuns. They're sisters. The photo was taken the day of their father's funeral in March 1959, in the backyard of their home in Dorchester."

"There's more," Roman said, and he gave Bridget a wink.

"I checked local road race results in the Dorchester area. Before she went into the convent, Delia Delaney volunteered as one of the organizers for Pop Gallagher's Dorchester A.A. team." Steele passed around a copy of a paper. "Here's a copy of the race results from a local race in 1951. As you can see, Delia Delaney signed it. And if you look at the picture of her we found, she's sitting at the registration table wearing a red hood."

Roman beamed. "So add it up. Delia Delaney signs a race result card. That makes her a runner. She's shown in the picture wearing a red hood. That makes her the runner we're looking for. Last but not least, go back to Freddie Norman's comment, that Finn called the runner in the red hood in the 1951 Boston Marathon 'Delaney.' What more do you want?"

"How do you know Delia Delaney is Sister Josephine's sister?" Bridget said.

"I checked city records and matched the number on the house with similar numbers in the neighborhood. The people who owned this house in this picture in the 50s were named Delaney. They had several girls in the family, one was named Delia and another Josephine."

"Plus there's more," said Roman. He gestured to Steele to share copies of his next paper, then Roman picked up the narrative. "Notice on this page, titled 'Birth Certificate,' the baby's name is 'Bridget Marie.' Bridget, that's you, and obviously this page is familiar to you. But you'll notice where it has a space for 'Birth Mother,' that space is blank."

Steele held back the next page, waiting for Roman to signal to him. When Roman gave him a nod, Steele passed out copies.

"Now, this is the important page," Roman said, continuing to lead. "I'm sure, Bridget, you've never seen this one before because this was not publicly available and it was difficult to locate, but we did find it in the records. You'll see this page is called a 'Consent

Form.' This is how things were done when adoptions were made back then and the mother wanted to remain anonymous. Note how the name of the baby is the same on this page, 'Bridget Marie,' but you'll see in space marked 'Birth Mother,' the name says 'Delia Delaney.'"

I looked over at Bridget and she looked as if she'd just been punched by Mike Tyson.

"That's how they did adoptions in 1952 when you were born," Steele said, underscoring the obvious. "The baby's name went on the birth certificate, while the consent form, which was recorded separately but not made public, showed the name of the mother who gave the baby away."

Roman, ever tactful, said, "Delia Delaney's your mother, Bridget. You'll have to send her a Hallmark when you find the Runner in Red."

It was all too much for Bridget. She walked to a tall window across the room and stood with her back turned. Jack walked to her and put his arm around her.

"Where did you get all this?" Bridget said in a firm voice as she turned back to Roman.

"We have our ways," said Steele, beaming like a perfect toady. "Would you like to talk to your aunt?"

"What?"

Again, Roman took the lead: "Sister Josephine is alive. She's in a nursing home in upstate New York, or so we believe."

Bridget's face showed another punch from Tyson.

"Where?"

"We don't have the address yet, but we will tomorrow. We will call you once we make confirmation. You can visit her and ask her for Delia's contact information, but Bridget," Roman paused for effect. "I need to wrap up this project. You've fallen a bit off the pace with your end of the investigation."

"I'll get it done."

"I need you to have Josephine put us in touch with Delia immediately."

"I know."

"Time is becoming a premium. I can't stress that enough."

"Don't worry about me, I'm going back to Boston tonight, but I'll drive to upstate New York tomorrow and get it done."

"Great," Roman said. "So there you go. I solved the mystery of the Runner in Red for you, now all you have to do is find her."

Jack caught up to Bridget and me on the sidewalk outside Roman's building after we left the meeting.

"It's hard to feel sorry for you anymore, Bridget, the way you're letting anger rule your life," Jack said, as he stepped in front of her, making her stop.

She looked him in the eye. "I'm trying to find my mother, Jack."

"You're letting anger rule your life."

"Anger doesn't rule me."

"Then why is revenge so important to you."

"I'm looking for my mother."

"Yes, so you can embarrass Pop. But Roman is the one getting the revenge, Bridget, on *both* of us."

He pulled out a copy of a running shoe advertisement from his suit pocket. She glanced at the page, but was unimpressed.

"I know all about this. So what if he bought a shoe company."

"He wants you to find the Runner in Red so the media will descend on Pop, showing how 'Pop Lied,' or some story along those lines. He'll showcase his shoes under the white-hot glare of that story—making himself the advocate for women first. Then you know what he'll do with you, he'll flip you—the way he'll flip the shoe company after he extracts his profit. I had him on 'Runners' Delight.' I know how he operates.'" Jack paused before continuing.

"But the real tragedy will be that you'll kill your relationship with Ellen, and for what good purpose?"

"I can never forgive you, Jack."

"What, for barging in on you two today?"

"No, for what you did to me with Ellen in Oregon."

This froze Jack in his tracks, and he was powerless to follow her as Bridget pushed past him on the crowded sidewalk, and I had to quicken my step to catch her.

"When are you going to the nursing home?" Stan said, as Bridget and I sat in her office at Channel 6 early the next morning. She kept eyeing the phone, as if that would make it ring.

"As soon as Roman calls with the address, we're going. I've got the car all gassed up."

"Ellen's running the New York City Marathon tomorrow, you know. She called a little while ago to ask if you would be joining them."

Before Bridget could answer Ellen appeared in her office doorway.

"Well?" Ellen said, but Bridget looked away. "You coming with us, Mom. Dad's in the car outside."

"And Pop?"

"He's in the car, too."

"I have a project, Ellen. And a deadline."

Ellen shook her blonde head, as if trying to shake off shackles that entangled her. "I can't believe it. I have a chance to win the New York City Marathon tomorrow and you don't even want to be there to watch me."

"I didn't say that, honey. I have an appointment."

The phone rang and it was Roman, on speaker. He gave the address of Sister Josephine's nursing home in a small town in upstate New York near Albany. But before he hung up he said, "Bridget, time's a premium."

Ellen handed a small box to Bridget after Bridget hung up with Roman. "Here's your Boston Marathon medal back, Mom. I went to Philadelphia earlier this fall to return it to you, but the delivery got side-tracked."

She shot me a look, none too kind.

"I gave this medal to you, honey, when you were in high school. It was my gift to you."

"And now I'm giving it back!"

Bridget took the box and slipped it into her pocketbook. Ellen turned and walked to the door, but Bridget jumped up from her desk and took a position in front of the door to block her exit.

"Wait," Bridget said, and the two stared at each other a long hard moment, looking like two champions from different eras dueling on the hills.

"Why should I wait for you, Mom, when you just showed me how easy it is for you to abandon me?"

Ellen brushed by her mom and I ran to catch her as she stepped out the station's front door, but she spoke before I could say anything.

"It's too late," she said.

"No, it's not. I can turn her around."

"I don't mean with her. I mean with *you*."

"Me?"

"You haven't done one thing to help. You haven't taken one step to turn her around like you promised me you would."

"And what about you?"

"Me?"

"Yes, you! I've become a damn marathon expert. It takes 41,600 steps to run a marathon, but you haven't taken one step toward me."

"Yes, I have."

"Every step is away. You need time, you say, but I've gotten calluses on my fingertips from all the times I've rung the bell at Pop's house to talk to you, but you don't answer."

"You want to talk to me? Fine," she said, and she pointed to the sedan where Jack sat behind the wheel and Pop sat in the back seat. "Come with me, you can talk to me in the car."

"I'll come. But I promised your mom I'd do something with her first."

"Oh, same bullshit," she said, and she elbowed her way past me. Then she climbed into the backseat with Pop and she didn't look back as the car pulled away.

"Does she hate me?" Bridget said, when I returned to her office.

"You *and* me."

"I'm sorry to entangle you in this, Colin."

"You can't hate Pop and love Ellen simultaneously, Bridget. Lines not parallel eventually cross and collide."

"You don't have to take this job with me anymore."

"No. I made my choice, and I'm in the middle now. Damn it, I'm not going to quit. But do give me the Maloney luxury of throwing a public fucking fit."

I slammed the door, hard. *Bang!*

The two receptionists at the front desk pretended not to hear and they smiled politely as I hurried past them on my way out the front door. But I didn't get twenty feet into the parking lot before Bridget caught me, and took me by the elbow.

"She's falling in love with you," she said.

"Hardly."

"I know my daughter. She wouldn't give a double-barrel blast to just any Joe."

I stared at her, letting the line sink in.

"Walk around a bit, cool off. I'll get the car, then we go to work."

CHAPTER ELEVEN

The tiny nun who greeted us Saturday afternoon at the door of the nursing home in the sleepy mountain town in upstate New York west of Albany lamented how beautiful Sister had once been.

"Like a little flower. She was so young. So pretty."

"I remember," Bridget said.

"But she's slipping fast and I don't think it would be wise for you to visit with her today." The nun told how Sister Josephine had experienced a rough night the night before and had been groggy all day. "Early morning is the best. Would it be possible for you to come tomorrow at 7 am?"

We told her that would be no problem and we stayed at one of those economy hotels. We made an early night of it and returned Sunday morning at first light. The tiny nun welcomed us and told us Sister Josephine was doing much better.

Technically Josephine's religious order did not have to accept her into the small brick nursing home nestled in the thick woods across from the Massachusetts line. She had quit the religious life in the 70s after an incident in Boston, but influential people from southern California—where she had worked for nearly a quarter-century teaching children in south-central L.A.—had made arrangements for her to return home to her order in New England, according to the tiny nun.

"You knew her well?" the nun said, as she led us to the second floor.

"She was my lifeline," Bridget said. "Is it Alzheimer's? I read the report."

"Yes, but she can be lucid. She has good moments and she had one in California obviously, because she told them she wanted to come home. Hopefully she will be lucid today. Don't be disappointed though if she doesn't recognize you. Her sister came to visit last month, but after she left Josephine couldn't remember the visit."

I looked at Bridget, who was thinking Delia Delaney—same as me—and I read the trepidation in her step as we entered Josephine's dimly-lit room on the second floor of the old house.

"Bridget!" said Josephine, who raised her head off her pillow and held out her hands. "Look! It's my dear Bridget."

The tiny nun put a hand over her mouth. "I can't believe this, she remembers you."

"Sister," Bridget said, and she took her mentor's hand, as tears appeared in both their eyes.

"This is a miracle," said the tiny nun.

Bridget stood beside Josephine's bed and touched her old friend's cheek. "You look wonderful, Sister."

"Oh, I've had a time of it," Josephine said, managing a smile.

"It's been so long."

"It has. Are you still mad at your father, dear?"

"Yes, Sister. Unhappily, I am."

"And he's mad at you still?"

"Yes, Sister."

She smiled. "You know what they say about an Irishman with Alzheimer's, don't you?" Bridget smiled that Sister could joke about herself. "They forget everything but their grudges."

"I can't believe this," said the tiny nun. "Wait till I tell Reverend Mother."

Bridget sat on the corner of Josephine's bed and they talked, mostly about how much fun they had had in high school.

"Did you do something with your talent, I hope?"

"I'm a television reporter."

Sister beamed. "Oh, good. You've won awards, I'm sure."

"I have, Sister. But..."

Sister had deep-set green eyes which were glossy from age and the effects of her illness. Her face was gaunt and deeply lined, but when she smiled at Bridget her eyes gained luster. "Yes, I know my top student. You've come to tell me something, yes?"

"No, to ask you, Sister Josephine."

"Please. If you've come to ask me, do."

Bridget glanced at the tiny nun, who nodded, yes, and Bridget handed Sister Josephine the photo of the three nuns.

"Oh," Sister said. "Oh, my!"

"Do you remember this?"

"I do. It was taken the day we buried our father, rest his soul."

"Is that my mother with you, Sister?"

A flash of light crossed Sister's eyes, but a hint of pain also. "Yes. It is."

She and Bridget stared at one another, a mountain of memories to match the mountains out the window, as Sister Josephine looked away. "I'm sorry I never told you."

"That's OK," Bridget said, and she took the photo back.

"Margaret never wanted us to tell you. I'm sorry if I hurt you by keeping her secret."

"Margaret?" Bridget said, and she handed the photo to Sister again.

"Is this my mother? Delia Delaney?"

"No, child. Delia's your aunt. Margaret is your mother."

"I'm sorry, Sister. I don't understand."

"Your mother, Margaret, is on my left in the picture. In the white robe. Delia and I have the black robes. Margaret is younger than me. Five years, ten. I'm sorry, I can't remember."

"Are you sure?" Bridget said, her eyes showing concern that she might be pushing Sister too far.

"I feel terrible I kept this from you when you were a girl in school. But that was Margaret's wish. She didn't want us to take any chance of hurting you."

Again Bridget hesitated before asking, "Can you tell me now?"

"Yes. Let me tell you everything. Margaret wouldn't mind, since Margaret's gone."

"Gone?"

"Margaret gave birth to you when she was sixteen. She was so young, so scared. Poppa was furious when he discovered she was pregnant. Delia agreed to put her name on your form. Not the birth certificate, but on the Consent Form. That appeased Poppa somewhat, since Delia was older, and it would eliminate the crime issue."

"Crime?"

"Yes. A girl, sixteen. Having a baby. Delia was nineteen. We tried to tell Poppa it was not a crime for a girl, but he wouldn't listen. He insisted that Delia be listed on the form."

"They altered my birth certificate?"

"No, they altered the Consent Form, don't ask me how. Poppa knew men at the firehouse who could get things done."

"Then what?"

"Poppa would not permit Margaret to stay in his house again. We had lost Momma to pneumonia two winters earlier and there was no one to placate Poppa. He refused to consider Margaret as his daughter anymore for the embarrassment she had caused him at the firehouse, to have a baby at sixteen. The way the men joked about it at the firehouse, playing him for a fool, not the firemen but the hangers-on."

"Who's my father, Sister?"

"I don't know. I never knew, dear. I think Delia knows. She might, since she offered to let them use her name. I'm sorry, it was so long ago, I'm sorry, I have a difficult time remembering everything."

"How did the Gallaghers get me?"

"Denis Gallagher offered to take you. That I know."

"Pop offered? "

"Yes. He knew Poppa from Knights of Columbus. He knew Poppa was in a fix, that he was going to make Margaret give up her baby, and Mr. Gallagher offered to help Poppa."

"He offered to adopt me? Pop did?"

"Yes. It was unheard of in those days, for a young girl to keep her baby after she got in trouble. I was at the convent then, and I don't recall much. But I remember Pop Gallagher came to the house one night and I was there. I remember Margaret's tears, and Delia comforting her. Mr. Gallagher offered to help, thank God for him, that at least you went to a family where I could watch you grow."

"So Pop Gallagher took me?"

"To help. You were sent to the Gallagher's and Margaret was sent out of the house by Poppa. She joined the convent, though she didn't join my order, or Delia's. She wanted to be a missionary, to go away. As far away as she could. She was headstrong about it. And we never saw her again, except for Poppa's funeral, and that photo."

"You said Margaret is gone, Sister?"

"Yes, dear. I'm sorry to tell you. Margaret is dead."

At that moment another tiny nun, older and more stooped than the first, walked into the room. She was round, with a pink face. She carried a tray with orange juice and a muffin. "Sister Josephine, I'm sorry this took so long with your juice."

But Sister Josephine continued. "Margaret became a missionary after Poppa banished her. She spent her life in El Salvador working in the missions, doing good for the orphans. She was killed during a civil war down there, when they raided her convent."

"I'm sorry, should I come back?" said the round nun.

"No," said the tiny one. "Not if Josephine asked for the juice."

"Sister, your juice is here."

"I didn't order juice," she said, looking perplexed. The weariness showed in her wan face despite the earliness of the hour, and Bridget leaned forward. She reached across the shriveled figure Josephine presented and touched Josephine's cheek.

"I'm sorry, I'm having a hard time remembering," Josephine said. "I'm sorry I can't be more helpful to you."

"We should step outside," the tiny nun said to me, and the round nun and I hurried out the door behind her.

"I'm sorry this had to turn out as it has," the tiny nun said once we were in the corridor. "Do you want Sister's juice?" "No," I said, as I continued to watch Bridget stand by Josephine's bed with her fingertips pressed against the sleeping nun's cheek.

The news that Pop had wanted Bridget shocked both of us.

"I can't believe it. He won't tell you any of this stuff?" I said as we got into her car, a Jeep Cherokee, and headed back to Boston along country roads in the early morning light.

"He never talks about me."

"Why not?"

"I don't know what motivates Pop, or has embittered him so deeply against me. But it's always been that way."

Again I could see why she had wanted so badly to find her mother, whom moments earlier we had learned was dead: she wanted to be released from a bitterness she did not understand.

It's interesting how a car ride as it goes along can promote conversation. It doesn't happen immediately, but a winding road such as the one we drove back along through the low mountains of New York creates a monotony that is relaxing. Eventually, like a stone skipping over the flat surface of a glassy pond, talk moves from mundane topics to issues of substance.

"You ever been in love?" Bridget asked me as the slanting light of the new day played along the undulating road.

"I'd like to be. With your daughter."

"I'm glad you're chasing Ellen. I hope you catch her."

"You do?"

"I know what it's like to want love and find it so elusive."

"You ever been in love?"

"I loved Steve Roman once. I believed I did anyway, which may be the same thing. I'm not sure. I know I should love Jack more."

"You don't love Jack?"

"I do, but I should love him more."

"Why did you go with Roman?"

"I don't know, it started in high school and lasted through college."

"You loved him?"

"Love, now, ah, there's a word. Steve was everything I dreamed of. A tight butt, of course, but I was attracted to him for his confidence, ambition, self-sufficiency."

"He seems like an arrogant son-of-a-bitch to me."

"I thought of it as self-confidence. I was such a young fool. A schoolgirl in love. But when I returned to my dorm room after the Boston Marathon in '71, after Pop blocked me, he was there waiting for me. He had a gaggle of news reporters lined up outside on the lawn, they all wanted to talk to me, and he had promised them he would set that up. I told him to forget it, I was in no mood to talk, but he said it would help him advance his career. I said forget it, I couldn't have been more emphatic, but he took my medal, the Boston Marathon medal in my pocketbook. Here, I'll show you."

She removed the felt box from her pocketbook where she had placed the medal after Ellen had returned it to her at the news station. She opened the case, showing me the 1951 Boston Marathon gold medal. 'If you're not going to go outside and talk to the group for me, then you can go out and get this,' he said, and he threw the gold medal out the dorm window. I found it in the grass in the rain as media types swarmed all around me."

I gave her a look like, wow, what a guy!

"I thought I loved him, but I realized he could love only himself, and that's the moment I saw his essence and woke up for good."

"Tell me about the medal."

"My mother, Pop's wife, gave it to me the night before she died. It was beside her bed, in this box. She told me my real mother had left it for me. I guess I should call her Margaret now."

"Why the hole in the center? There's supposed to be a diamond in the middle of the Boston Marathon gold medals, right?"

"That's true."

"But yours doesn't have a diamond."

"It was missing the diamond when Pop's wife gave it to me."

"What happened to it?"

"I never knew, and Mrs. Gallagher didn't know either. It's a mystery. One of the endless mysteries surrounding Pop and me."

We sped along, still the only car on the road, as we left New York and the sign in the thick trees said, "Welcome to Massachusetts."

"Where did the medal come from? I checked it out and that medal has never been on the open market."

"I don't know. Pop had forbidden my mom, his wife, to talk to me about my past, even after I learned I was adopted, and of course she never disobeyed Pop. She was such a sweet, unassuming woman, Mrs. Gallagher."

"Does Pop know where the gold medal came from?"

"Undoubtedly. He knew my mother was Margaret, right?"

"But he never told you anything about her?"

"Pop has never cooperated in any matter that would benefit me."

"Why not?"

"Because I tampered with the immutable laws of nature, Colin."

"Just because you wanted to run?"

"No, because I am a woman."

I didn't say anything, though I sensed her trouble with Pop went

104

deeper.

"That's why this search for my real mother has been so important to me. I want to know where I came from. I don't value myself fully, yet I want to desperately. I don't know who I am and that separates me from others. I want to connect to people on a more intimate level and end the isolation I feel that separates me from other people—I want to feel whole—but now that chance is gone. Margaret is dead."

I didn't say anything, neither of us did, until the car engine made a clanking sound and Bridget said, "What's that?"

"Do you put oil in this thing?"

"Not that I know of, what oil?"

"Engine oil," I said, as we clanked and bucked, and rolled slowly to a stop. At least I was thankful for the blink of an eye small town we were passing through as the engine seized and the car cut out. A moment later we came to a stop in front of a sign, "Weathervane Inn, South Egremont, Mass."

"What's happening?" she said.

"Car died."

"Oh, now isn't this shaping up to be a banner day."

CHAPTER TWELVE

Clapboard houses faced a church with tilted gravestones at one end of the town, while a country inn, the Weathervane Inn, sat along a curve at the other end of South Egremont. We went inside the inn to find a phone when the proprietor, a voluble and animated sort, approached us at the door. He introduced himself as Vinnie, a refugee from the corporate world of Manhattan.

"Since this is the last weekend for foliage, it'll be a two-hour wait for brunch," he said. "But you can go to the bar to wait and get coffee."

Bridget made a motion like "charge," and said, "To the bar, but not for coffee," while I looked for a phone to call Triple A.

"You won't have luck with that," Vinnie said. "Hank's gone to the bank."

"Bank?"

He made a motion like casting a pole. "A fishing bank."

"So our stellar luck continues," Bridget said, as she climbed up onto a stool and ordered a double scotch.

"Massachusetts law, I can't serve you before noon on Sunday," said Vinnie, and Bridget gave him a pained look.

"She just found out she lost her mother," I said, glancing at the clock that said 9:30 am. "Anything you can do, Vinnie, to help us."

Truly he was a refuge from Manhattan who understood cosmopolitan ways because he made a searching motion as if looking for cops, and said, "I don't suppose the Mass Alcohol Bureau agents will be out at this hour hunting for offenders," and he poured her a double.

"Excellent, kind sir, thank you. We'll drink, then think," she said, as she motioned for me to take a stool beside her at the bar.

"How bummed are you?"

"You mean to learn that my mother who I've been seeking for more than twenty-five years is dead? Or that my car won't start?"

"I'm sorry, I didn't mean to sound flip."

"Colin, you're a great kid. Just order a drink, OK? I can't handle anything else at this point."

She tossed her drink down and ordered another, which Vinnie poured. I got the sense, car or not, we wouldn't be heading back to Boston any time soon.

"Ellen left," she said, after her third drink. "She did not write or call."

I got the feeling that this was going to be a particularly painful day, especially with the New York City Marathon set to happen later that morning and us, being hundreds of miles away. I signaled to Vinnie for a beer while we waited for 10:40 am and the start of the race so we could watch it on TV. What the hell, if Hank was at the bank, what was I doing playing Bridget's mother?

"It began with my going to San Francisco. No, actually it began before that, in high school, when I had to choose between Jack and Steve. Do you want to hear about this?"

Before I could answer a man in overalls walked in, the inn's maintenance man, asking if we were the owners of the "broke down" car. "You want me to call Preston in Great Barrington? It's Sunday, but Preston might be at Sunoco? He could look at it."

"Yes," Bridget said, and she slipped him a twenty. "You do that and we'll do damage equal to the car."

"After the incident with my father and the fall-out with Roman over the medal I was ready for a change," she said picking up where she had left off. "So I moved to California in June 1971. I wanted to get as far away from Boston as I could. Frisco—they hate it when you call it that—was 'happening.' Everyone wore flowers in their hair and their libidos on their sleeves. That was my wild period."

Vinnie tuned in, an ear cocked, but an elderly couple walked to the bar and interrupted.

"We're here to celebrate our 50th wedding anniversary," said the wife, a round woman with a feathered hat and heavy eyeliner. "We're up from Brooklyn to do the day justice," she added, loud enough for all of Massachusetts to hear as her husband, a beanpole with a bad toupée, nodded.

"Certainly," Vinnie said and he left to check them in.

"I found a job in an art gallery in the Fillmore district," Bridget said, hitting stride again.

"Then one night more than two years later as I sat on the couch in my tiny apartment, safe from the 'anything goes' action on Sacramento Street below, drinking Anchor Steam from a quart bottle, smoking a joint and watching the Mary Tyler Moore Show, a knock came on my door. 'I got a question for ya,' Jack said. It was Jack, all the way in from Boston, wearing cutoff jeans and a Red Sox t-shirt. He smelled from the beers he had thrown down over the last hundred miles on I-80 before reaching the coast. Colin, you with me?"

I nodded, while Vinnie, who had returned, listened also.

"'I come to getcha, Bridget,' he said. 'But I got one question since you never answered any of my letters. Will you marry me?' Jack said. So I did. We left that night in his Pacer and Ellen was conceived in a sleeping bag somewhere between a Wyoming Hot Shoppe and an Ohio Turnpike plaza called the 'Blue Heron.' Prosaic, huh?"

"Hardly prosaic with a name like 'Blue Heron.'"

"We got married in Boston, seconds before I showed. It wasn't fireworks, but Jack's a good guy. He's tops in his office in Waltham. Sells insurance. You need a policy?" she said, killing her drink.

"What about Ellen?"

"Ellen's birth made it all worthwhile," she said, tapping the bar for another, and Vinnie was Johnny-on-the-spot. "Her life gave my life purpose."

"So you loved her?"

"Of course I loved her. I had what every woman wants, Colin, a chance to make a perfect child."

I thought maybe that overstated it. "Some people have dogs and they're happy."

"I never said I have perfected being a modern woman, Colin," she said, throwing back her glass. "The thing I loved most about being a mother was the control I had over this new person. I could shape Ellen's life and instill values I considered important. Things I had missed in my own life. I could prepare Ellen to deal with the world in a way that I was not capable. Am I making sense?"

She didn't wait for my answer.

"It was similar to the control I had over my body when I had been a runner, the hard work and sacrifice, and I relished the responsibility and the challenge."

"What went wrong?"

"Wrong?" She looked at me crookedly. "You think anything's gone wrong?"

"I mean," I said, but she laughed, that wonderful laugh.

"You're perceptive, Colin. That's why we pay you your paltry salary."

"Why did you hire me?"

"What?"

"If your purpose was to have a perfect child, a job you're fucking up royally, pardon the expression, why do you need me?"

"You want another beer?" Vinnie said, and I accepted, as I waited for Bridget's answer, but she ignored my question.

"Ellen was a bright baby. And she did well. Too well. Too early in any case. It's not that I didn't want her to run. Jack says I never wanted her to run. But that's wrong. I didn't mind her eclipsing me.

That's what Jack called it, my opposition to her, he said I was afraid she'd eclipse me as a star, but that's a hundred percent wrong. That's just Jack being bitchy."

"Bitchy?"

"Yes, bitchy. Jack agreed to let Pop train her for the Olympic Trials when she was a sophomore at BC, though I knew she was too young. 'She can get hurt,' I told Jack."

"What happened?'

"She got hurt, of course. She loved running, from the love Jack had for the sport, and from Pop's love also. Which is OK, that Pop took an interest. But Pop took too much interest."

"Now who's bitchy?"

"I know it sounds like sour grapes, but I disagreed with Pop training my little girl so hard when she was so young. The newspapers wouldn't let go of it, though. They loved the connection, that Ellen was following in her mother's footsteps. But Ellen is a pure girl, with a pure heart, and she got mixed up in a misguided sense of loyalty, as if she owes Pop, which is what he plays on."

"She's smarter than that."

"Pop's bad for her. He's pushing her, for his own purposes, so he can win the Boston Marathon through her, but she's the one who will pay the price, believe me."

"She can handle stardom."

"I'm not talking about stardom. Ellen accused me of trying to direct her life, but despite her histrionics I refused to support her. Then she got hurt, like I predicted, and she married that empty suit."

"Crutchfield?"

"Yeah, let her tell you about that zero sometime. I'm not going to discuss miniature Romans. But I was devastated when she announced she was getting married, leaving school and moving away. First to Florida, with her child-husband, then after they broke up, to Oregon to try again for that track team out there. Then of course Jack had an opinion, he told me, 'Your problem is you can't have a daughter with spark and not think she's not going to want to leave a mark.'"

"A mark? Hell, it's dangerous out there!" I shot back.

"Then, sure enough, she got hit by a car and whatever wheels were left on the wagon with Jack and me rolled off. Where's the ladies' room?" she asked Vinnie, who she sensed was listening, which he was. He pointed down the corridor and she got up.

"Whoof. She Irish by any chance?" said Vinnie, and I nodded.

"Mind if I turn on the TV? I've got a nephew in the New York Marathon today, and it's about time for the start," he said.

"No, do that, please. We want to watch it, too."

When Bridget returned, walking a little shaky, there was a commercial on and she continued with her story.

"The next day I read a story in *Runner's World*, which is how I kept in touch with Ellen's life. Can you believe it? That's how I kept in touch with my daughter, through a magazine. The article said Ellen had nearly been killed by a hit-and-run driver three months earlier."

"Three months?"

"That's right. I hurried to Waltham to show Jack the story, but he had a look on his face, and I knew."

"Knew what?"

"That he knew already. For God's sakes, even Pop knew. Jack had kept it from me. Unbelievable. He would fly out there on a regular basis, supposedly for work, and he never told me."

"What did you do?" Vinnie said, pouring himself a scotch.

"I got on the next plane, with Jack in tow. By then Ellen was out of the hospital and I found her lying on a couch watching Seinfeld reruns, sobbing."

"'Why didn't you tell me?' I asked her.'"

"'I'm a failure,' she said, sobbing.'"

"'No, you're my daughter.'"

"'I never wanted you to say I told you so.'

111

"'Oh, baby,' I said, and I told her I would take her home. But she refused. Then Pop wrote her a note, offering to train her, and she came back to Boston, only after he wrote to her."

"Is that the hardest part for you?"

"He took my life away, now he was taking my baby again."

"That's why you're so mad at Jack?"

"I can never forgive Jack for permitting it."

"Another one?" Vinnie said, answering her signal as she rapped the bar with her wedding ring, hitting it hard.

Then the commercial ended and the picture cut to an aerial view of the Verrazano Bridge in New York as ABC Sports' coverage of the 1999 New York City Marathon began, and I watched Bridget's face fall.

CHAPTER THIRTEEN

*B*ang! went a gun—a cannon—at 10:40 am, and we watched on the screen above the bar as 26,000 runners exploded onto the bridge with the force of a dam bursting.

A cheer rose from the runners with the cannon's smoke and mixed with the chopping air as dozens of helicopters whirled overhead in the gray blowing sky. The runners spilled forward in a continuous stream and the flow rolled up the long slope to the bridge's crest, then down again toward Brooklyn, and the New York City Marathon was underway in the morning light.

I glanced at Bridget to see how she was doing, and though hardly sober, her face took on a pensive expression and she became very quiet.

"You all right?" I said, and she nodded, engrossed in the race, yet the change in her was not unlike a car going from 90mph to zero after hitting a wall.

A trio of reporters in the studio bounced the commentary to Amby Burfoot, Editor of *Runner's World*, who rode in a motorcycle side-car in front of the lead pack of male runners. Amby gave a report on the men's race, then the ball was bounced to Kathrine Switzer to do the same for the female leaders from her motorcycle side-car. What fascinated me was to see Pop sitting in the side-car with Kathrine. ABC Sports knew the irony of the pairing, I'm sure, to twin Pop with Kathrine who, in the years since Jock Semple and Pop had chased her down the road in the 1967 Boston Marathon, had

113

parlayed her fame into becoming not only an advocate for women's running globally, but a famous sportscaster.

As she and Pop talked back and forth about the women's field—including Kathrine highlighting the presence of Ellen Maloney, America's "Comeback Gal," in the field—I was reminded of the story about John F. Kennedy's inauguration. It had always fascinated me how the skipper of the Japanese cruiser that had rammed JFK's PT boat in the Pacific during World War II—nearly killing the president to be—rode second in the parade behind the new President and Mrs. Kennedy that day, as if in some way he had played a role to make his enemy president. Which he had, and I suppose Pop had, too, in terms of the running game, played a hand in making Kathrine famous. He had helped (along with Jock) usher in the thing they both had fought to stymie—women's running. Now Pop was a color commentator on the women's race. Ah, the world!

"I don't see her, Pop, do you?" said Kathrine, meaning Ellen, as the lead pack comprised of a dozen runners from ten countries—none of them America—passed the four-mile mark.

"Don't worry," Pop said. "She's in there."

We listened as Kathrine, red hair flying in the wind, told how the women in the lead pack—including the two favorites, Rita Turganov of Russia and Sonia Nita of Kenya—had come out of the gate fast and after four miles the group was ten seconds ahead of record pace.

"It just goes to show how far women have come in a short time," Kathrine said. "That the leaders can buck a headwind like this and still run at this speed."

"Where is she?" I asked Bridget, whose eyes were glued to the TV, but she said, "Pop's right, she's OK."

I blinked to make sure I had heard that correctly. Was that a compliment she had just paid Pop?

"I see her," Kathrine shouted ten minutes later after Amby's report on the men's race and the coverage bounced back to her.

"I just saw the lead American with my binoculars," Kathrine said.

114

"Ellen Maloney, the one everyone calls 'Comeback Gal.' She's three hundred yards back, not quite a quarter mile, running in 18th place."

A camera picked her up along Fourth Ave. in Brooklyn and we got our first look at Ellen. She was moving with a sea of bodies, everyone with their heads high, chests rising and falling, as the colorful runners formed shifting patterns, like the images in a kaleidoscope. They came up the street in a steady stream, knees churning, arms swinging, feet crunching Gatorade cups, moving fluidly in comparison to the wild, pulsating crowd. Ellen looked comfortable in her red top and black shorts with her blonde ponytail swinging back and forth like a pendulum in perfect time across her shoulders.

I glanced at Bridget for more insight, wanting it badly, this being my first big race. I wanted some indication about what I should be feeling—positive or negative with Ellen so far back—but Bridget 's face was hard to read—seemingly devoid of emotion—but yet full of emotion, and she was too engrossed to talk.

"Don't worry," she said a moment later, a delayed reaction to my question. She took a pen and scratched figures on a napkin as the lead group of women—reduced now to seven—passed the eight-mile mark and plied through Williamsburg. I watched as Bridget performed a calculation taking the time off the screen, 44 minutes and 4 seconds, with Ellen 300 yards back, translating that into a split time at eight miles of 45:03 for Ellen.

"Good for you, Pop," she said, under her breath and I stared at her. Was that *another* compliment?

"Ellen is not a fast starter," she said, looking at me for the first time in nearly an hour—a time during which she had downed three more scotches. "I want her to run her own race, not the leaders.'"

"What did you mean, 'Good for you, Pop?'"

"You know how I feel about Pop, but he knows his stuff. He's holding her back till they get through Queens, till they come off the 59th Street Bridge onto First Ave. in Manhattan. That's his plan, I'm

115

sure, to hold her back, then have her pour it on, use the downhill coming off the bridge to drop in a fast mile or two and work her way back into the thick of things."

"Get me on, get me on," Kathrine shouted into her headset as the lead group of four women—the Kenyan, the Russian, a German, and an Ethiopian—came off the 59th Street Bridge onto First Ave. "I got movement in the women's race!"

The camera cut to First Avenue and Ellen became visible suddenly, 50 yards behind the women leaders, as they made their way up the boulevard. She was unmistakable in her red top and blonde ponytail, and she was moving fast, eating up large quantities of real estate that separated her from the four in the lead.

The roar of the million-plus crowd, thickest on the East Side, offered a thunderclap for the first women, which included Ellen now, who continued to inch closer.

"She just dropped in a 5:09 mile," said Bridget.

"Is that good?"

"Damn good! Come on, honey!" Bridget said, tapping the bar for another hit and Vinnie responded.

Ellen poured it on, and I gained a new appreciation for the term as she passed the runner in fourth, the German who flagged and continued to slide back. Over the next two miles Ellen moved into a tidy spot behind the trio in front where she let them break the headwind as the group navigated through the Bronx before making the turn back into Manhattan.

"5:11," said Bridget. "Blistering again. So smart, so smart to save her strength for the end like this."

Bridget's excitement was reflected in Kathrine's call on the race. Kathrine highlighted how rare it was for a runner to make up so much ground—giving Pop credit for training Ellen to be able to come back like this. Kathrine continued to tell and retell the story of how Ellen had, at one time, been the brightest young runner in America before hitting hard times.

"But as we can see from the signs along this course today, this crowd loves their 'Comeback Gal!'"

The lead group of three entered Central Park at 102nd Street with Ellen one stride behind them. The group ran three abreast and Ellen showed signs she wanted to make a move, but she did not.

"Smart, honey," Bridget said. "Hold on, just a bit more!"

"What do you say, Pop? Can she overtake them?" Kathrine asked.

Pop, who sat beside her in the motorcycle, his white hair blowing, said, "You know the rules. I can't coach her out here like this, but she knows what to do."

And it was as if an oracle had spoken because suddenly Ellen moved and a great cheer rose from the crowd along the winding path through Central Park. They cheered lustily as Ellen swung left on the narrow road and moved off center, off the blue line that showed the way, and edged around the other three women, taking them by surprise as she grabbed the lead.

"Oh, we've just had a move by Ellen Maloney!" Kathrine said. "But, wait, the other two are answering."

Nita from Kenya and Turgenov from Russia, the two favorites, gave spurts and caught Ellen again as the Ethiopian fell back. Now Ellen was running three abreast with her two main rivals, her blonde ponytail flapping frantically.

"Oh, what a race for the ages," said Kathrine. "We've never had a women's race as heated as this."

Then as the trio exited the Park onto Central Park South—a mile and half to go—the Kenyan and Russian made a move, as if in concert. They edged closer to the curb, forcing Ellen who was on the inside to shorten her stride. Ellen took a stutter-step, missing a beat, and she fell back two yards behind Nita and Turgenov, who—again, as if acting in concert—gave it gas and opened another two yards, then five yards, as the group passed the 25 mile mark with a mile and 385 yards to go.

"Now, she's third, Ellen Maloney, and oh, it looks like she's fading," said Kathrine. "She may be out of gas after her hot pursuit over the last ten miles."

I looked at Bridget, her face jammed with emotion, but holding herself in control.

"Is she OK?" I said, totally out of control.

"Will be," Bridget said, taking a hit on her scotch. "Come on, baby!"

And Ellen was OK. As the trio turned off Central Park South at Columbus Circle and entered the Park and the final straightaway, Ellen swung wide off the blue line again, gave it a spurt and made an effort to circle around the two who ran shoulder to shoulder and catch them by surprise.

"Oh, what a move," said Kathrine. "Where, oh, where did Ellen Maloney get the energy for that little engine blast?"

Turgenov and Nita missed it, and Ellen moved into the open space and widened her lead as the crowd went wild. She continued to stretch her lead as the throng leaned in from both sides, looking like a political convention with all their "Comeback Gal" signs being thrust up and down in the chill gray air.

Then with two hundred yards to go and Kathrine calling this the greatest finish ever, Ellen appeared to trip, just slightly, but enough that Nita and Turgenov took advantage, and they pulled even again.

With one hundred yards to go, the trio ran three abreast and all the easy action of their arms and the steady piston-like motion of their strides vanished. It was a mad dash as Nita moved out front first, then Turgenov followed, and Ellen struggled to hold on down the final stretch, fifty yards, thirty, ten, five, and that's how it ended: Nita, Turgenov, Ellen, one, two, three.

Nita, the winner, Turgenov, second, and Ellen Maloney third, all of them in a time of 2:25.05, as Kathrine shouted into the mic:

"Oh, you'll tell your grandkids about this one, folks, because today you just saw a finish for the ages!"

CHAPTER FOURTEEN

Vinnie was the first to speak.

"Wow, that's gotta be a heartbreaker. They all finished in the same time, but it's gonna be hard for the girl who got third to live with that. I better go check on the dining room."

Bridget sat stiller than stone, staring into space, and I sat beside her without saying anything, letting the impact of Ellen's loss sink in.

"You folks ready for brunch?" Vinnie said when he returned from the dining room. "Things have thinned out nicely in there."

"What time is it?" Bridget said.

"Not yet 2," said Vinnie. "Wow, what a finish. You guys ever seen anything like that?"

Bridget didn't answer, instead she said to the open air, "Jesus, I'm polluted!"

"You know when our car will be ready?" I asked Vinnie.

"Dexter says tomorrow about noon. But there's a bus to Manhattan that leaves out front at eight tonight if you need to get back to a city that bad."

"You got a room?" Bridget said, as she stood, doing an imitation of the Leaning Tower of Pisa.

"Actually, we do. One just opened up next to the couple from Brooklyn. With foliage, we've been so slammed."

"I gotta lie down," Bridget said. "You got a nightgown?"

"We have Weathervane t-shirts. Some people use them that way. If you take a large size and stretch it."

"Gimme," said Bridget, swaying. "Where's the room?"

Vinnie grabbed a key and a t-shirt and showed us the way up the stairs. "Wow, what a race," he said again. "But oh, that poor girl who got third!"

"I'm hurting Colin," Bridget said, as I held her arm and we followed Vinnie up the stairs.

"You'll be OK," I told her.

"I lost my mother and now I've lost my daughter."

"She'll understand."

"She'll throw a hip-shits that I wasn't there."

Vinnie looked at me for an interpretation.

"She means a shit fit."

"Oh," he said, and he kept climbing, but Bridget paused to catch her breath and we all stopped.

"She'll never forgive me for missing that, Colin."

"She already did a hip shits on you, at the news station—you'll be fine."

We arrived at the door to our room and Vinnie opened it. He gave me the key and Bridget made a beeline for the bathroom after Vinnie gave her a Weathervane t-shirt.

I waited for her, half expecting to hear heaving, but the woman was an iron lady, and all was quiet. Until she came out, dressed in her Weathervane t-shirt, her gorgeous legs on full display. She went right for the closest of the two beds and lay down. Crashed is more like it. She cut a still figure, but hardly a serene one, with her legs curled up under her in a fetal position. I sat down on the bed beside her, but she was gone, passed out, and I engineered the covers deftly to get them out from under her legs and slide her in between the sheets.

"Colin?" she said, waking up as I pulled the covers over her shoulders. "Will she always hate me?"

"She doesn't hate you."

I tried soothing words, but it was like throwing seed on rock as she shook her head, resisting my attempts to comfort her, then she passed out again, and I took her hand as she slept.

It was about half an hour before the knocking on the wall began, and I wondered if it was pipes, until I realized the couple from Brooklyn had shifted into high gear.

For several hours I sat beside Bridget, watching as the wall next to us vibrated and the sky turned darker out the window in stages, waiting for 8 pm and the bus. I used the time to think back over all my experiences with Bridget, from the *Runner's World* she had brought to the office in Philly, to her parking her car across from me on the street in Dorchester the night she told me she wanted me to work with her on Runner in Red, to "run with her," as she had called it.

But my favorite Bridgetism? Hip-shits!

How could it not be!

Soon the clock on the desk showed five to eight, so I tucked her in one more time, tight as I could, and I ran for my bus to New York and hopped on as it pulled to the curb outside the Weathervane.

It was after midnight by the time the milk-wagon of a bus made all its stops and arrived in Manhattan, and another half hour by the time I made it from the Port Authority Bus Terminal to the Sheraton on Seventh Ave. where Jack had reserved a suite for Ellen, Pop, and himself. Since the hotel was near Central Park, I took a detour and checked out the marathon finish line. A few bikers and kids on roller blades breezed by over the big word, "Finish" painted in the street. All was dark at that hour, but the energy of what had happened in this spot earlier that day and the thousands upon thousands who had streamed over the spot following the dramatic finish in the women's race remained, and I soaked in the majesty of that energy and Ellen's gutsy achievement before going to the hotel.

Jack let me in. I had called from the bus and left him a voice message that I was coming, and he greeted me at the door with a big Irish hug.

"Ellen and Pop are sleeping," he said, as he invited me into the dark room. "But I set the couch for you."

As I lay on the couch, curled inside a thick comforter from the closet, I lay awake listening to the quiet, punctuated by muted car horns on Seventh Avenue far below and I wondered why Bridget and I were so alike. Why did we both hold life at arm's length? It was not a thought that came immediately, but one that crept into my brain as I floated suspended between consciousness and sleep, the hum of the heater droning on, and after a while I was dreaming, or thought I was, when I sensed a warm figure kneel on the carpeted floor beside me.

"Colin?"

"Huh?"

"Can I come in?"

"Uh huh," I said, and I moved over on the couch.

"Thank you for coming," Ellen said.

"Oh, hey, yeah. By the way, you did great."

"I'm still not ready, you understand, don't you?" she said, whispering, as she slid in under the covers beside me and touched my cheek. "Not yet, OK?"

"Uh, huh," I said, still half asleep. "Stay back, stay back."

She chuckled, then she said, "Sorry I was such a bitch the other day."

"You were fine."

"Hold me?"

"Yes," I said, and I pressed back against the couch to make a bigger space for her in my arms. She wore a t-shirt, one of Jack's white t-shirts with nothing under it, and I could feel how warm she was. "Your mother watched you today."

"She did?"

122

"Every second of it, glued to the TV."

"Thank you for doing that."

"No, it was her, Ellen. All her."

"Will you wait for me?"

"I've got a question. Do you like me for me, or because I can be helpful to you?"

"What are you talking about?"

"That day on the river, you said I could be helpful to you with your mom. Do you like me because I can be helpful, or because I'm me?"

"I carry your baseball card in my wallet, does that answer your question?"

"I'll wait for you, long as you want."

"Thanks for coming tonight," she said, and she kissed me squarely on the lips, moist. I held her tightly one more time, then she slipped away out of my grasp, and a moment later her bedroom door closed. I lay in that spot a long time, pressed against the back of the couch, the impression of her breasts against my chest a warm sweet memory.

And I convinced myself, as the car horns played softly on Seventh Avenue below, that her visit had not been a dream and Bridget had been right: She was falling in love with me.

CHAPTER FIFTEEN

After replaying the tape of the dramatic finish, the host of the *Today* show, pulled up a chair to face a couch with the three top finishers of the women's division. He congratulated Nita and Turgenov, then asked Ellen if she minded falling just short.

"No, because it was a great race."

"You appeared to stumble in the last hundred yards or so. Was there a pothole? Did the City fail to fix a hole on the course?"

"No excuses, it was a great race."

"Do you have any plans for the future?"

"Certainly."

"I mean races. Have you picked your next race?"

She patted Pop's knee, who sat on the couch beside her. "My grandfather and I are going to win Boston in April. That's our big one, I want to win it for him. I look at yesterday and my contest with these two great ladies as a tune-up for our next match."

"So there you have it," the host said, turning to the camera. "Ellen Maloney. A true champion from the old school. She runs because she loves it and she knows where she going."

The Klieg lights went off and the host made small talk with the group as a gaggle of technicians helped Ellen off with her wires and she gave hugs to Turgenov and Nita. I stood to the side, planning my day deciding what roads I would take back to Boston, especially now that I had been asked by Jack if I would take the car and drive Pop home while he remained in New York with Ellen.

Roman blew in at that point with a dozen acolytes in tow, including ponytailed men and big-haired women, all in power suits. I watched them come through a side door, and I watched Roman signal to them to wait. As he stepped gingerly toward Ellen, Jack glared at him, but Jack did not block him, though I thought he might and certainly could have.

I couldn't hear what Roman was telling Ellen, who listened politely, but he was highly animated—pointing to his group who all waved in unison—and she nodded, awkwardly yet politely still, and I assumed he was outlining some big PR plans since I kept hearing "L.A. this, L.A. that."

I looked at Pop, who wore the same stoic expression he had as he rode in the motorcycle side car with Kathrine Switzer, but as Roman's group pulled out cellphones setting big plans in motion, I felt Ellen slip away. I recognized this as the first brush of a current that would pull her along, then sweep her up in the rising tide of fame, and as I watched. I realized Ellen didn't belong to us any longer. She belonged now to something larger, the whole world, and I knew her life would never be the same again.

The break in the clouds at the end of the marathon Sunday had continued overnight, giving us a brilliant fall day on Monday as I drove Pop home. Past New Haven Pop asked if I'd pull off Interstate 95 and pick up the old Route 1. I was enjoying his company as he told story upon story of the old days and I savored that I had the "Casey Stengel of Running" as my private tutor.

My favorite story was the one about "fear the man with a paper bag." Pop told how Jimmy Henigan, a plodder colleague who won Boston in 1931, used to say, "Pay no mind to the man with the dime store uniform. Fear the man who brings his running gear in a paper bag, that's your real runner."

I got off I-95 at Old Saybrook and we wended our way to Route 1, a two-lane road that hugged the Connecticut shore. Pop told me this was the road he had taken when he had first emigrated to America from Galway and had hitch-hiked during the 1930s to Boston from Philadelphia for the Boston Marathon each April. He had been a carpenter in Philadelphia, when he could get work, and he lived in a rooming house in South Philly on nuts and tomatoes from the trash bin at the farmers' market.

A faraway look appeared in his eye as he peered down the road, alternately turning his head side to side to see if anything remained the same. "There, there. Stop!" he said.

I pulled over in front of a tiny stucco structure with a flat wooden canopy held up by two rusty metal poles, an old gas station. Today it was a t-shirt shop and God knows what else it might have been in between.

"I spent two days and a night here in '36," he said, when the tiny structure had been a gas station. He got out and I followed. We went inside the t-shirt shop where a long-haired hippy in a Led Zeppelin t-shirt sat behind a picnic table and said, "Howdee. Any special kind of t you want? I got a Mo Vaughn, or you want something from my Rock 'n' Roll line?"

Pop didn't hear him as he shuffled through the cramped room, turning his head in all directions, surveying the place from top to bottom, while I explained to the fellow who looked like the guy on Zig Zag rolling paper that this was Pop Gallagher, former director of the Boston Marathon, and this was a place where Pop had stopped while hitching to Boston during the 30s.

"Cool," the guy said, and I saw he was not absorbing any of it, having gone one toke over the line himself many years back.

In the car as we drove again, Pop told me how he had been stranded at that gas station without any money and that had cost him his chance for gold at Boston.

"Several papers in Boston had picked me to win in '36. I had consumed my fruit I had brought, since the journey had taken me longer than I expected, nearly a week, and I was famished."

"It took you a week to hitch from Philly?"

"Yeah, and I helped the owner by pumping gas to earn 75 cents so I could buy some food and eat at least. Finally, a salesman going to Boston pulled in for gas and offered to take me the rest of the way. His car had the old isinglass curtains instead of windows, so there was no seal on the window beside my shoulder and I froze in the car as we drove all night. The salesman took me to the start at Lucky Rock Manor because I was so far behind schedule getting into town and we arrived just before the noon start. The salesman was a heavy-set sort and never exercised, but he admired the 'plodders,' as we were called, and he offered me $5 if I promised to win the Boston Marathon for him. But of course, I couldn't take it."

"Why not?"

"Because we were amateurs and that was against the rules. If I had taken money, I would have been barred from running again, ever."

"Officials would have had to hear about that first."

"Those were the rules," he said, flatly.

I nodded and he continued.

"I led for the first half, but I cramped in Wellesley. My legs were still tight from riding in the cold all night. Then Tarzan Brown caught me on Heartbreak Hill, just before he caught Old Kel. I caught Kel too, on Beacon Street in the stretch, but I cramped again before the turn onto Exeter Street, and Old Kel caught me again for second place. I got third."

"Did it bother you, that you never won?"

"Yes, but that won't be a problem come April. When Ellen wins."

I realized the depth of his pride, and the source of his desire. I understood why he worked so hard to help Ellen, so she might participate with him in the writing of the final uncompleted chapter of his life.

"It will be a great honor," he said, adopting a faraway gaze. "To have my kin do what I couldn't do."

I was shocked and I glanced at him to see if he considered the irony.

"Bridget's your kin, too, if you look at Ellen that way."

He turned to me with a fire in his eyes I had not seen, and had only heard about in stories. I saw in his expression an anger that made me shudder. It was as if I had pushed a boulder to the brink of a cliff and it teetered now, a thousand feet above ground, over my head.

"Don't mention that name to me."

He had awakened my competitive juices, however, and I felt like I had when I played ball and we were down by one run in the ninth with one chance left to bat.

"Why? Why do you hate Bridget so much?"

"Hate's not the word."

"Then what?"

"Bridget thinks about only one thing," he snapped, and he turned away as the car rolled past a dozen white stripes in the road, and I waited for him to give me the missing piece. "Bridget thinks only about Bridget."

"She gave you credit for training Ellen."

He looked at me. "She said something about that?"

"During the race yesterday she told me, 'Pop knows his stuff.'"

"She said that?"

"She gave you credit for Ellen's strategy."

I had pushed the boulder dangerously close to the edge, but now possibly I was rolling it back. But no luck.

"Don't talk to me about that ingrate," he said, and the rock rolled away from the precipice, but something else rolled away as well: I sensed the connection between us snap as we rode the final fifty miles to Dorchester in silence. As I pulled to the curb in front of his house to let him out, though, he leaned back into the car and spoke softly, as if all his air had been expended—except for one last bit.

"Tell Bridget thank you."

"I will," I said, and I waved good-bye.

Neither knows how to say they're sorry, Ellen had said. Old Irish, which I knew something about myself.

But, hey, maybe we were getting a thaw.

Nope!

I got a call from Bridget as soon as I checked into the station the next morning. She was in New York, following up with Roman to report on our visit to Sister Josephine and share news that Margaret was dead.

"I want to keep Roman on our side," she said.

"How many Tylenol did you need?"

"Several cases, but both the car and I are OK. Now let's get back to work. Roman just shared with me that they found Delia, and I need you to get her on tape."

"Found Delia?"

"Yes, she works in the cafeteria at a middle school in Dorchester, at the Washington Irving. I told Stan to give you a camera and a truck. I need you to get over to that school, Colin. And when you do, call me, I'll talk you through the interview I need you to do with Delia Delaney."

"But if Margaret's dead, doesn't that end all this?"

"You're in the news business, Colin, you should know better. We never go with one source."

The school was located on a hill, across the street from wooden houses, once stately, which sagged now under scraggly brush. Behind the school's chipped gate the lawn had turned to dirt and the brick walls of the tired building carried indecipherable messages from various gangs. I rang the bell on a metal door and eventually someone answered, a stooped custodian, who pointed in the direction of the cafeteria.

"What's the news want?" said a heavy-set woman in an A-line dress who spotted me with my camera in the basement hallway. She stepped in front of me at the entrance to the cafeteria as she directed the flow of kids barreling down the stairs for lunch.

"Are you the principal?"

"Assistant principal. What's up?"

"Tell her we want to talk to a lady in the caf," Bridget told me over the cell phone, which I had on speaker so I could take directions. "Tell her we want to talk to Delia Delaney."

"Who's that?" said the AP, meaning on the phone.

"My boss. Bridget Maloney. Channel 6 News."

Her eyes widened disapprovingly. "Listen, I don't care how many Oscars or Tonys you guys have won. You need to go upstairs and sign in at the office before I can let you down here."

"Tell her we need to ask Delia Delaney a few questions," Bridget said, but the AP heard Bridget over the speaker and shook her head.

"I can't help you. We got rules."

"Who wants to see me?" said a stout woman. Tall, with a stern, bony face, she stepped out of the cafeteria into the hallway and glared at me as she ran her palms along her white apron. She was in her sixties with broad shoulders and gray hair. She wore a hairnet and beads of sweat had collected on her brow from serving lunch.

"Ask her if she knows Pop Gallagher," Bridget said.

"Do you know Pop Gallagher?" I said, and the stern woman's eyes showed shock, as if I had picked her up and set her back two spaces on the black and white tile floor.

"No," she said, but I know when someone is lying.

"Look, you've got to go upstairs," the AP said, blocking me. "We've got rules."

"Get her on tape, Colin," Bridget said, and I raised my camera and pointed it at the cafeteria lady, but she was strong and she put her hand over my lens and pushed the camera away.

"Ask her if she ever had a niece," Bridget said, and I could tell from her tone on the phone Bridget knew things were not going well.

The stout woman heard Bridget, and she turned away. She stepped hurriedly back into the cafeteria and closed the door.

I went to follow her, but I had to jump back to let a group of kids rush by me into the cafeteria, including the kid from the sporting goods store, the one with the Mariners cap, which he wore backward still.

"What's happening?" Bridget said.

"The kid," I said.

"What kid?"

"From the shoe store," I said, as the kid scampered past, turning over chairs as he dodged other kids in a game of "Got you last."

"That's Samuels," said the AP. "One of our lesser angels."

"Do you know we caught him stealing recently?"

"Yes, I do, sadly."

"How did he get readmitted to school so soon?"

"'Released into parental custody,' they call it," she said.

"What?"

"The parents vouch for them, in his case his guardian, and if our Principal signs, which ours did, we take them back. The juvenile courts are jammed and we keep them here before their hearings."

"You're kidding?"

"No, our principal has taken a special interest to help that boy."

"What's going on?" Bridget said. "Where's Delia Delaney?"

"She's gone."

"Gone?"

"Look, I'm sorry," said the AP. "But if you want to come down here, talk to the Principal upstairs and get permission. Otherwise, I've got to ask you to leave."

"Whose policy is that?"

"School policy. You need a slip."

"No, I mean the 'parental custody' thing?"

"You think I make the rules? Go upstairs and ask them. They get paid the big bucks, I just enforce the rules. Look, I've got to get this area cleared out before the next crowd hits on third lunch."

Bridget who was following the action on the phone told me to get my camera running as I climbed the stairs. "Get the principal on tape. I want her on record giving you permission to interview Delia Delaney."

"Excuse me," I said, as I entered the Principal's office, a cramped, cluttered room on the main floor, filming as I came. The principal, a spry, elderly woman in a floral dress, stood with her back to me. She was speaking on the phone, arguing with downtown administrators for funds. She hung up, and I focused in tight on her eyes, capturing her shocked expression when she turned to me.

"Can I speak to you?" I said, filming.

"Yes, certainly," she said, her voice more tenuous now than it had been moments earlier on the phone. "What do you need?"

"Ask her to call Delia Delaney to the office," Bridget said on the phone.

The woman looked at the phone in my hand, then at me, as I honed in tight on her blue eyes.

"I have Bridget Maloney, Channel 6 News, on the phone," I said. "We'd like to speak with Delia Delaney."

"Who?" the woman said.

"Delia Delaney."

"No, on the phone?"

"Bridget Maloney. Channel 6 News."

"No," she said, and I was put off, not by her refusal as much as by her tone, the finality of it.

"What's going on?" Bridget said.

"She said no."

132

"She can't say no. We have a right. Tell her."

I told the principal. "We have a right."

"No," she said, again, shaking her head, and she covered her eyes to escape the camera. I believe I saw a tear.

"Why not?" I said, anticipating Bridget.

"This is not the way," she said.

"We have a right," I repeated, again anticipating Bridget.

"Look," Bridget said. "If she won't give you a permission slip, ask her this question. You said you saw that kid downstairs. Ask her how she let someone who stole from a store back into school."

"She didn't. They have a policy." I couldn't believe it, here I was locking horns with an elderly principal over a permission slip, while arguing with my boss in New York.

"Just do it, damn it!"

"Why did you let Samuels back into school?" I said, but still the woman shook her head and waved her hands in front of her face.

"What's so special about him?" Bridget said.

"What's so special about him?"

I saw tears well in the old woman's eyes, real tears, and suddenly I felt like I was back in Philadelphia with the Food Bank director grabbing my ankles.

"What's going on?" Bridget said. "Did she give you the permission slip yet?"

"No," I said, and I turned my camera off as the woman buried her face in her hands crying.

Good lord, I said to myself. What am I doing here?

The elderly woman turned to me, looking twenty years older than when I had walked in. She followed me to the door where she caught up to me and with her composure restored, but with tears in her eyes still, she fixed me with clear blue eyes and said, "All my children are special to me."

"What's going on?" Bridget said. "What's happening?"

"Nothing," I said, and a moment later I was out the front door and heading back to the truck, as Bridget badgered me to get back in there and get them all on tape.

"You're not going to use this tape, I hope," I said on speakerphone as I drove back to the station.

"Damn right I'll use it. I've already called Stan. We're going to show how one school is harboring a criminal."

"But it's not the principal who makes policy. You can't put her on the air for letting the kid back in."

"You're missing the point, Colin. The point is leverage."

"Put her face on TV tonight and you'll ruin her career."

"I damn right will put her face on TV if she doesn't give us a permission slip to talk to Delia Delaney."

"You'd do that?"

"You bet, then watch how fast they call tomorrow with the slip."

When I reached the station, Junior met me at the door asking what I had from the sporting goods store.

"Oh, Christ, what does Junior want?" Bridget said.

"Who's that?" said Junior.

"Bridget," I told Junior. "I got her on the phone."

He took the phone out of my hand. "Maloney, does your boy have the tape you shot with the girls in track shoes last week?"

I could hear her clearly. "Colin's got great stuff," she said, and I knew what she meant.

"Get in there and edit the piece," Junior barked at me. "I want to make 5:30 with your story."

I hung up with Bridget and walked to the editing suite, but as I sat in front of a monitor the phone on the desk rang. I picked it up. It was Bridget from New York again.

"Grab the tape," she said, and I reached for my camera.

"No, not that one," she said as if she were psychic. "The one from the running store."

I was proud of her as I found the tape we had shot at the Prudential Mall and I worked quickly, mixing images of young girls bouncing on their toes in their "Women First" shoes. Bridget was silent on the phone as I worked, but I knew she was following the progress.

"Done," I said.

"Good. Give it to Junior. And thank you."

"The girls will enjoy seeing themselves on TV."

"I don't mean thank you for that. I mean thank you for catching me before I destroyed an innocent old lady."

I smiled. A moment later she said, "Colin? You still there?"

"Yes," I said, smiling ear to ear. I was happy I had made my choice to stick with her.

Bridget doesn't think only about Bridget.

CHAPTER SIXTEEN

The knock on my apartment door came in the dark, past midnight, and it woke me with a start.

The rap came again, this time more insistently, and I was shocked to see Ellen standing in the doorway in her running clothes.

"What are you doing here? I thought Roman and his crowd had swept you away to L.A. for a promotional gig."

"Roman plays my mom like a harp, not me. Will you run with me?

"In the middle of the night?"

"I came to find the guy on this card," she said, and she handed me my Red Sox rookie card, the one she had bought for three bucks. "I came on my bike. You take the bike. I'll run beside you."

I slipped into a pair of running shorts and pulled on a sweatshirt, but she said, "Whoa!" as she stood hands on hips looking at the huge poster-size photo of her I had hanging over my bed. The photo showed her breaking into the lead over Nita and Turgenov in the New York Marathon, and the headline said, "Here Comes America's Comeback Gal."

"What's *that*?"

"What's what?"

"That picture of me on the wall!"

"Oh, that! That was the back page of the *New York Post*. I took it to Kinko's and had them blow it up big. Gives me something to remember you by."

"You're crazy!"

"Crazy about *you*!"

"You're embarrassing me!"

"I'm promoting you. You don't need Roman and his minions."

"Let's go, before I return that baseball card."

We took off up Dorchester Ave., she running fluidly on the sidewalk, blonde ponytail flapping, me biking along the curb next to her. The street, usually chock-a-block with traffic during the day, was devoid of people at this hour except for the occasional wino. We glided along smoothly through Edward Everett Square and up to the junction where Dorchester Ave leads to Mass. Ave. when suddenly she stopped in front of an all-night Dunkin' Donuts.

"Can we go in here?"

"You want a donut?"

"Pop can't see what I eat when he's asleep. Plus I want to talk to you."

We sat in a pink booth in a back corner of the neon-lit shop. I opened the conversation as we sipped coffees and ate chocolate donuts with sprinkles.

"You never told me why you got married," I said.

"After I got hurt in the Olympic Trials, I was afraid to stand on my own two feet."

"That's insane. You didn't fail. You were a kid, not yet twenty. That was just your first sortie into the big time."

"You're very wise."

"You should listen to me. I'm the poster child for fucking up young. What was he like?"

"One day while we were living in Florida, he dropped a phone book in my lap. He said, 'Turn to any page, you'll find one of my girlfriends.'"

"Wow, he tormented you like that?"

"He was into control. I was no good to him if he couldn't break me."

"And you broke?"

"I did. But I had enough left to start divorce proceedings before I moved to Oregon. I went out there to try for a comeback with Nike. I enrolled at The University of Oregon in Eugene, but my running wasn't going well. I had lost my zip, and the other girls kicked my butt. It was very competitive and I stopped going to my classes. My ex dragged his feet on the divorce, and I started piling up 'F's'. Soon everything fell in on me. Then the team cut me and I went out for a long run in the middle of the night. I was in the woods, nobody around, when a car hit me and sped off. A group of hunters found me by side of the road in the morning."

"How long did you lay there?"

"Four hours, five, in the rain with the temperature in the 40s."

"Jesus!"

"I had never been lower in my life, and I wanted to give up living until Pop wrote me his note."

"The one about sending your ships to sea?"

"He saved my life, to have that kind of confidence in me. He truly believed I could be good again."

"You proved that at New York."

"Thank you. Do you think I can do it at Boston?"

"Without a doubt."

"Should we hit the road again? I want to show you the place where I'm going to banish the demons."

We continued up Mass. Ave. until we got to Boylston Street, then she motioned to me to turn right onto Boylston, and we continued along the nearly empty street until we came to the Boston Public

Library, a place I recognized from all my trips to the building for research.

"Stop," she said, as we pulled up to a spot that had faded letters in the street spelling the word, "Finish."

"This is where the media bridge goes," she said, making a sweeping arc with her arms as I set my bike on the side of the road. "This is the finish line for the Boston Marathon. The bridge with all the cameras creates an arch above this space."

"This is home plate for you, isn't it?"

"This is where my life will culminate come April. All I need to do is get it done, get across this line. Then all the demons will be gone."

"You will."

"Running against Nita and Turgenov, it's always a fight against the part of me that wants to be a coward."

"Playing at the top, it's a pressure cooker, I know."

"There are a hundred places you can give up in a marathon, but in every race it comes down to one moment, make or break, where you have to resist the part of you that wants to be a coward. I did that in Oregon, I gave up, but I don't want to do that anymore, give up."

"When Nita and Turgenov pulled ahead of you down the final stretch Sunday you could have broken, but you came back against them. You showed real grit. I don't care that you got third, in my mind you were the winner."

"What do you call it in baseball, 'Stay back?' I don't want to do that anymore, fail to be all I can be."

"The thing I loved about baseball is how one moment you can make an error and be a goat, but the next moment make a great play or hit a homer and you're the hero. It's a wonderful concept, redemption."

"I need to redeem myself after New York."

"No, you don't! You're worthy all by yourself. That's why I'm out here in the middle of the night, in the freezing cold, to be with you—because you're *you*."

"Maybe we should call it 'Step up.'"

"Let's do that. We'll relegate 'Stay back' to the ash pile of history."

"I like your idea of redemption."

"I saw you Sunday, gritty girl. I have no doubt you'll get it done."

She smiled. "Can I take you home again?"

"Only if I get to practice my singing."

"What are you talking about, singing?"

"You get to be Katharine Ross to my Paul Newman."

I showed her how to climb up on the handlebars of the bike and as she sat with her back to me, I gave her a ride the way I used to ride Happy Donovan and Jerry Raskopf home from our ball games when we were kids. As we pedaled along heading south—she facing front—I sang the words to "Raindrops Keep Falling on My Head" as we rode.

"You're crazy!" she said.

"Crazy about *you,*" I said, and I kept singing.

I pedaled along, all the way down Dorchester Ave. to Fields Corner, singing all the way and she couldn't put her hands over her ears because she had to hold onto the handlebars.

The shower in my apartment was a tiny metal surround, very much like a tin can.

"No more stay back," I said as I held her and she held me.

"Step up, step up," she said, and we took turns undressing each other. Soon we were kissing under the warm spray, holding each other, her with her pink skin and blonde hair, and me savoring the moment, and we took turns soaping each other.

Clank, clank, clank went the tin can of a shower as we bathed under the spray before moving to the bed.

It was warm under the covers which flew off the bed at intervals before we pulled them back over us again and wrapped ourselves in them and each other. It went like that for a long time, until the first light of the new day in the window got our attention.

"I like 'step up,'" I said, as I pulled the covers over us for another go.

"Here comes Comeback Gal," she said, and I gave thumbs up to the big picture of her hanging over my bed as she wrapped her long golden legs around me one more time.

The next few weeks passed in a blur and all I remember is being happier than I could ever imagine.

Events transpired in a blur: the election was held and Governor Finn won in a walk. Then Thanksgiving came, which we celebrated with Bridget and Jack—everyone on their best behavior—at Bridget and Jack's white center-entrance Colonial house on a tree-lined street in Wellesley.

I even got Bridget to get me a break from work so I could go out to Colorado with Ellen over Christmas where several of her teammates from the Nike team in Oregon had moved to continue their training. She was big news in the running world after her New York City Marathon race and they invited her to train in Boulder with them. She was eager to get altitude training under her belt, and to see her old friends. It was great for both of us to get away. We got some mountain time in the snow, though she didn't ski—for fear of risking injury—but I did, to test my ankle, and my ankle, like everything else in my life at the moment, felt just fine.

It was mid-January when I returned to Boston, while Ellen remained in Colorado to step up her training with her friends. I was eager to see Bridget and work with her again. She had calmed down in her pursuit of the Runner in Red, largely, I believe, because she questioned the point of it all now that she had learned Margaret was dead and Delia didn't want to be found. Delia had quit her cafeteria job with Boston Public Schools after our visit to her school—me with the camera and Bridget on the phone—and she left no forwarding address.

Bridget didn't talk about it, but I think another part of the drop off in her enthusiasm for the Runner in Red was the boost in confidence the race in New York had given Ellen.

Though Bridget didn't say it explicitly, she had become a fan of the "Pop and Ellen Show" and was as eager as everyone—including the national media and the whole country in the aftermath of the New York City Marathon—to see the "Comeback Gal" get another shot at Nita and Turgenov at the Boston Marathon come April. There was an excitement in the air that was palpable, building for that rematch and the chance Ellen would have to rewrite the script of the New York City Marathon finish.

I sensed Bridget wanted to support Ellen and everything was going in that direction including at work where Bridget took on mundane stories, and we didn't talk about the Runner in Red any longer.

"You have the names of the streets?" Bridget asked me late one afternoon in early February after I'd been back from Colorado a few weeks. I drove along the perimeter of Logan Airport in the van as she sat beside me, and we worked on a story about new traffic patterns at the airport.

"I do," I said, and I pulled to the side of the road to start our shoot when the phone rang in the van. It was Stan with a call that was about to change everything.

"Bridget, you sitting down?" he said, and she put him on the squawk box so I could hear.

"I'm on a roadway outside Logan Airport for chrissakes, Stan.

Where am I going to sit?"

"Well you better find yourself a seat."

"What are you talking about?"

"I'm holding a note for you."

"Yeah?"

"From your mother."

"What?"

"She wants to see you."

"What are you talking about, Stan?"

"One of the guys from the maintenance pool in the garage out behind the studio here. He just came in with a note. He said an elderly lady handed it to him this afternoon. She asked him to give the note to you."

"I'm sitting down now, Stan, I'm back in the truck. Tell me what's going on," she said.

"The guy was working under one of the vehicles, changing the oil, when the elderly lady walked into the garage and slipped the note under the truck for him. She said, "Give this to Bridget Maloney. Tell Bridget her mother wants to see her."

"Oh, my God, really? You think it was Delia Delaney?"

"No, the maintenance guy said her name was Margaret. Your mother's alive, kiddo!"

We turned to each other simultaneously, both of us wearing OMG faces!

CHAPTER SEVENTEEN

Here's what the note said:

Dearest Bridget,

I have longed to see you for so many years. I was overjoyed to have had this time in Boston these past few months to watch you on TV and watch Ellen with her marvelous running, including trips I took to Hyde Park to sit in the stands and watch her practice. I was doing my best to work up the courage to contact you, so I could see you in person, but something has come up and I don't know how much longer I will be able to stay in Boston. They believe I'm in danger. I don't give a hoot about that, but I have been successful to this point buying time. I am trying to work out details with the law enforcement man and I have urged him to let me stay until the Boston Marathon so I can watch Ellen run. But I don't know if I will be successful with my pleas. That is why I have taken this chance to reach out to you now. I want to see you before they take me away, I want a chance to hold you in my arms, and I will be in contact again to see if that can be arranged.

Love, Margaret

"Wow!" we all said in unison, as Stan, Bridget and I sat around a table in Stan's office and read the note a hundred thousand times. Junior walked in and asked what we were doing.

Bridget slipped the note between her knees, pinching her knees together, and we all said, "Nothing," in unison.

But Junior knew something was up. "I hear there was some kind of commotion with the guys in the maintenance pool. Do you know anything about what's going on?"

"Not that we heard," said Stan.

Junior left and I turned to Bridget, "What do you think?"

"Tim Finn," she said, and I knew what that meant.

Time to get back in the car.

We found Tim Finn at the Governor's Dorchester office on Gallivan Blvd. across from the Erie Pub. Bridget showed him the note from Margaret and he was as shocked as we were.

"What do you make of it, Tim, her point about the 'law enforcement man?' What's that all about?"

"I have no idea, really."

"No more obfuscating, Tim, talk to me! Does this law enforcement thing have anything to do with the trouble you were in in the old days?" He shook his head, but she kept pressing. "Talk to me, Tim. Were the Delaney sisters wrapped up in that legal mess with you in any way?"

He looked her in the eye and his response was clear: yes.

"Tell me," she said. "No more holding back."

"I was at the City then, as you know, at the Child Services Office. It was a simple process and we had a system, Delia and Josephine collected names of worthy families in Boston that could not have children and your mother supplied the babies. I did the approvals for the adoptions."

"Supplied? What do you mean supplied?"

"Margaret ran a mission in El Salvador, during one of those civil wars they were having down there. She was the Mother Superior."

"When was this?"

"She was in El Salvador the whole time she was in the religious life, but this would have been the late 70s. That was her passion, helping babies. Delia and Josephine were nuns in Boston. You know that because Josephine was your teacher."

"Right," she said. "Keep going."

"It was selfless work they were doing, saving babies. The three of them, three good sisters, asked me to help. Margaret, your mother, needed homes for the orphans who would have starved otherwise. The army was killing the parents of the children, and sometimes even the babies got caught in the crossfire. It was a bad scene, but Margaret put herself in the middle of it, to find an escape for the babies. Delia and Josephine came to me at the City to ask me to help Margaret, and how could I say no?"

She stared at him.

"Each time Margaret had a baby to save, Josephine and Delia would find a family in Boston. I did the paperwork for the adoption, and your mother would send the child. They needed to move the babies quickly, sometimes very fast, and I would do the paperwork outside protocol to expedite things. That's what happened when I assigned a baby to a bad guy. You know all about the bad guy from the news stories, right, and the time I did in prison?"

Bridget nodded, prompting him to continue.

"The operation shut down after that, and both Josephine and Delia left their orders. Josephine moved away, California. I don't know where Delia went after she left her order."

"The baby that got abused by the bad guy, as you say, was that one of Margaret's babies?"

"Yes, Delia and Josephine were the conduit from Margaret to me and I made the adoptions official. But the one with the bad guy

I rushed too fast. The sisters didn't do anything wrong. The man was evil, they couldn't know that. They were only trying to save babies, the three of them. The babies would have starved without their attempts to intervene, but I made sure the paperwork for the bad guy who hurt the baby showed up as my error."

"You covered for them?"

"Yes. Five years at Walpole was easy for me compared to the guilt they carried for something that wasn't their fault."

Bridget walked to the window and looked out. She stood with her back to Tim as she absorbed all that. I watched Tim Finn's face, half expecting to see him crumble, but a new light shone in his lidded eyes, as if a heavy weight had been lifted off his shoulders.

"You can see why I couldn't talk to you when you came to Hyde Park High last fall."

"Where is she now, Tim? Where is Margaret?"

"I don't know, honestly I don't."

"She wrote me this note in the last twenty-four hours. She's someplace close by."

"Like everybody, I thought she had been killed by the thugs who raided her convent during that civil war. This whole time, I thought she was dead, like everyone else, we all believed that."

"You wouldn't lie to me, Tim, please not now?"

"I'm telling you the truth, Bridget, I swear. We all thought she was dead."

"I'm going to need to come back to you for more."

"That's fine, and I will help you. But let me ask you one favor. Do this thing, find your mother, but do it in a way that you don't take Pop down, OK?"

"I agree. There's no sense involving Pop."

"Why don't you talk to Young John. He was closest to Jock Semple. He might have information from his end at the B.A.A. He may know something about Margaret that can help you."

"You're a strong man, Tim."

"I'm not, Bridget, but thank you."

"Where to now?" I asked Bridget after we returned to the car.

"We're going to take a cab ride in Connecticut."

New London is a small town on the Connecticut shore. Old, brick buildings, warehouses during the whaling days, had been converted into malls with shops like J. Crew, while restaurants with nautical names on shellacked wooden signs occupied renovated storefronts. Early the next morning we drove to New London and found Johnny Kelley—"Young John"—hanging out in a taxi queue at the Amtrak station in a 50s Buick turned Yellow Cab.

"Bridget," he said. "I got your message you called. What's up?"

"I need your help, John."

"I was about to run this sailor out to Foxwoods so he could make a donation. Hop in."

"Hell, I don't do donations," said the sailor, all of twenty and shorn of all his hair. "I'm the ace of Black Jack in Tennessee."

"See what I mean?" said Young John. "A donor. If you don't mind taking a ride to the casino, we can talk."

We made an incongruous picture: the shorn sailor sitting in the back of the cab with me, counting his bills, while John J. Kelley, America's best runner from a quarter century earlier, drove his sister's cab. The cab company, with the single cab, was his sister's company, but Johnny Kelley enjoyed driving part-time—"to rub elbows with characters," he said—after he retired as the town's most beloved schoolteacher. Next to Johnny in the cab rode Bridget, America's first elite female runner, who peppered him with questions about a nun from El Salvador.

"Nobody on Jock's team talked about nuns. But they did talk about things that would have gotten them into trouble with the nuns," Johnny said, exercising his sardonic wit.

"I can imagine. Anything else you remember about the 1951 Boston Marathon?"

"As I told you when I saw you in Boston, the '51 race was important to Jock and your dad, especially with the Japanese sending over a strong team. Everybody in America, all the guys who fought in the War, were rooting for an American team to carry the day. Both Pop and Jock wanted to be heroes by winning the team prize. But when it came to Pop and Jock they'd combine events in countless ways to create a storyline favorable to them, you know that. So 1 never knew who to believe."

"You ever hear the name 'Delaney' mentioned?"

"I don't recall ever meeting anyone by that name, but I do know there's a Delaney on a plaque at the Hyde Park VFW Hall."

"What plaque?"

"The Hyde Park race in March, '51, a month before Boston, was the only time the D.A.A. beat our B.A.A. for the team prize in a run-up to the marathon. To rub it in, those D.A.A. guys had a plaque made, a big one, with the names of all the runners on their team, and they hung it in the VFW Hall. Every March we had to go to that Hall for the final tune-up before Boston and that plaque would stare us in the face. The four Finn brothers' names were on it, but so was the name 'Delaney.' Staring at that plaque year after year, that's not something you forget."

"When we gonna be there?" said the sailor, as he finished counting his money again, this time sideways.

"Soon enough, lad, for you to make your contribution," said Johnny, then he paused before he turned back to Bridget. "There is another thing I remember about 1951. I remember Jock got hot under the collar at Pop about a particular bill. They were both co-directors and equally responsible for the operation of the race. I remember Jock calling out your dad for allowing a double billing for the gold medal that year."

"Double-billing?"

"Yes, the B.A.A. had been billed for two gold medals and Jock wanted to contest the bill, claiming it was an error. The diamond on that medal can get expensive, as you know, and Jock was frugal. But Pop told him not to worry, he'd take care of it. Their discussion carried quite a lot of heat."

We turned a corner and came upon the Foxwoods Casino, a garish faux palace in the middle of the woods, the sight of which lit the sailor's eyes as bright as the lights on a slot machine.

"Stop!" he shouted.

Young John pulled to the curb to let him out and the kid paid John, but the sailor shoved the change into his pocket without offering a tip.

"See," Johnny said, with a wink, as the sailor sped through the chrome doors to do his business. "Your old man and Jock were two of the simpler characters I've had to contend with in my time."

The VFW Hall sat in the middle of a busy thoroughfare in Hyde Park. The building, a sagging brick structure with a small yard in severe need of weeding, was located down the block from a tired town center. Tim Finn was waiting outside as Bridget and I pulled up and parked in front of the hall.

"Good of you to come, Tim," she said.

"I'm as eager as you are to ensure Margaret is OK."

Inside the hall, an old man with puffy eyes sat behind a desk in a flannel shirt, blowing smoke rings. His name was Smokey McKee, the custodian of the building.

"Hey, Finn," he said. "Great news about your brother winning again."

"Thanks, Smokey. You don't mind if I take a moment to show these folks around?"

"No, not at all. Your brother hiring yet?"

"Sorry, Smokey, he's got his team in order already."

"Tell him I need a job, Tim. Something that pays more than this, with benefits."

"Keep doin' what you're doing, Smokey, guarding the Dunkin' Donuts, you'll be OK."

The main room looked like an extension of the 'marathon museum' in Pop's house with road race pictures all around. Tim gestured for us to follow him to a wall across from Smokey's desk. On the wall was a plaque dated, "March 1951," with a list of names, including, "M. Delaney."

"My mother?" Bridget said.

Tim nodded, as the cell phone in Bridget's purse rang. "What, Stan?" She nodded, then folded the phone and put it away. "Junior," she said to me.

"What's up?"

"Stan thinks Junior senses something," she said, and she turned to Tim again. "Keep going, what about the plaque?"

"Sit down," he said, and he pointed to a couch. "Let me tell you a story."

We sat on the couch as he pulled up a folding chair.

"A girl, blonde, prettiest blue eyes I'd ever seen, she lived around the corner from me in the Uphams Corner neighborhood when I was eighteen. She was just sixteen, and she asked me if she could run with me as I jogged to Fields Corner one afternoon. Of course, I said yes, though that was unheard of, a girl running in the roads. But she was fast, fast as me almost, and we hit it off, especially when I learned she was my girlfriend, Delia's, kid sister. Then one day she asked if she could run a race with me, and I thought she was kidding, but I thought, hey, this could be a kick. Hyde Park was the final tune-up before Boston that spring in 1951, and Bailey, our fifth man, had a pulled hamstring, so I let her run."

"You let her run on Pop's D.A.A. team?"

151

"You need a shot, Tim?" Smokey said, as he held up a bottle of Jameson.

Tim waved him off as Smokey poured himself a drink, and Tim continued to tell us everything.

CHAPTER EIGHTEEN

I waited outside security at Logan Airport for Ellen who was flying back from Colorado that evening.

My heart skipped a beat when I saw her and it jumped again when she waved to me with both hands high above her head. We were holding each other tight in baggage claim waiting for her luggage when my eye caught a banner for the 10 O'clock News, "Exclusive to Channel 6," on the TV above the carousel.

"Whoa!" I said, "What's this?" The picture cut to a shot of Steele standing outside the VFW Hall in Hyde Park. He had Smokey standing beside him.

"We are live in Hyde Park with a story based on a tip offered by this gentleman, Francis 'Smokey' McKee, who says Pop Gallagher, the epitome of integrity at the Boston Marathon for nearly thirty years, lied about circumstances surrounding the first woman to run a marathon on American soil. Tell us, Smokey."

"I was dustin' the trophy case, like I do every day, when I seen the plaque, the one you got in your hand there, and it all just came back to me. I said to myself, 'I don't remember Pop's D.A.A. team ever having a regular runner named, 'Delaney.'"

"Who's *that*?" said Ellen.

"A saint we met this afternoon. *Jesus Christ!*"

Smokey continued: "So I checked into it and I realized 'M' Delaney was the sister of a girl, Delia Delaney, who used to help Pop with race administration."

As he spoke the TV showed photos of the D.A.A. team from the 50s, including the picture from Roman's office of Delia sitting at a race administration table wearing a red hood.

"Delia was Tim Finn's girlfriend and she had a kid sister named Margaret who wanted to run."

"Pop's rules precluded women from competing," said Steele. "Why did Pop let a woman compete on his team?"

"It was Finn's idea. The D.A.A. had a man, Bailey, who was injured, and Finn let Margaret Delaney replace Bailey. He put her in a red hood, a sweatshirt he borrowed from Delia, so neither Pop or Jock would see the subterfuge. Oh, she ran like the wind and beat half the men. Pop's D.A.A. beat Jock's B.A.A. in that big Hyde Park tune-up for the Boston Marathon because of her."

"Continue," said Steele.

"That's how Margaret got her name on the plaque. Finn put it there, 'M. Delaney,' just her initial. Imagine, the same thing Kathrine Switzer did 16 years later, signing her initials, 'K.V. Switzer' on her application for the 1967 Boston Marathon. It worked for a girl in 1951, too."

"Amazing," Steele said, "Tell us, how did Pop Gallagher lie?"

"You fellas pay for this information, don't ya? There's some kind of compensation?"

Steele nodded vaguely, enough to prompt Smokey to continue and as he spoke, the picture showed war scenes from the Pacific theatre in World War II.

"At the 1951 Boston Marathon, the Japs were still smartin' from losing the war and (bleep). Oops, can't say that on TV, I guess. But the Japs planned to win the team prize to make up for getting bombed and (bleep). Sorry, force a habit. Both Pop and Jock wanted their boys to hold off the Japs, but Tim Finn convinced Pop they needed 'M.' Delaney on the team. Pop went crazy when he heard 'M.' was a girl, but Pop wanted to win the prize very bad, so he let Tim Finn put Delia's red hood on Margaret, and Pop let her run in the '51 Boston Marathon. That's how Pop Gallagher knowingly permitted the first girl to run in the Boston Marathon, and he's been lying about it ever since."

The screen showed Freddie Norman's picture of the runner in a red hood on Heartbreak Hill in 1951, then the shot cut to Steele for the close.

"So there you have it. Tonight we know that Pop Gallagher, staunchest defender of the rules against women—a man who once blocked his own daughter from crossing the finish line—permitted the first woman to run in the Boston Marathon, a woman named Margaret Delaney in 1951. This makes Margaret Delaney the first woman to run a marathon in America and calls for a total re-writing of the history of women's running. This has been a Channel 6 exclusive."

"Where did he get all *that*?" Ellen said, as she stood frozen in baggage claim, her hands covering her mouth.

When we got to Pop's house, a huge crowd including several news crews had formed on the sidewalk, along with the kid on the bike.

"Like in the movies, old dude's been holed up in there for hours," said the kid.

We edged our way through the crowd making our way to the front door, where we were joined by Bridget. Ellen glared at her mother.

"You did this!"

"No," Bridget said. "This is not what I wanted."

"You created this situation," Ellen said and she pushed her way to the front door, where Pop opened the door just a notch so Ellen could squeeze through as two or three news reporters thrust microphones under Bridget's chin on the front porch.

"Ms. Maloney, what can you tell us about Pop's lie?"

"I'll kick his ass," she said, turning on her heel, and I knew what she was talking about.

"I tried to hold them off," Stan said, when Bridget and I got to the station.

Junior stood beaming in a corner of the newsroom.

"Wait till your father hears about what you did," Bridget said, but he smiled even wider.

"My father ordered this."

"He what!"

"You never could cross the finish line. Those were my father's exact words."

She shook her head in total disbelief.

"How does it feel not to be in bed with my father any longer."

I never saw it coming, it came so fast, her hand as she whipped it around and slapped Junior full in the face, leaving red marks on his cheek from the outline of her fingers.

"You little twisted turd piece of crap!"

I rushed out the door to catch her as she hurried to her car.

"Where are you going?"

"To New York, to confront him, and I'm not even stopping to catch a plane."

She spun pebbles as she pulled her car out of the parking lot and took the turn onto the main highway on two wheels.

Back at Pop's house, I stood on the sidewalk out of the way of the crowd, which had grown larger even at that late hour and I tried to get Ellen on her phone inside. But she did not answer.

"When do they start shooting?" said the kid on the bike.

"Don't you ever go to bed?"

"And miss all the action? This is better than anything on TV," he said, and I watched as he pedaled up and down the block looking for fresh angles in the crowd to observe the action.

That's when my phone rang and I thought it was Ellen getting back to me. But it was my brother's wife Rosemary.

"Colin!" she said, nearly hysterical.

"Rosemary? What's up?"

"It's Kenny, Colin!"

"What about Kenny?"

"He's been shot!"

"What?"

"In the back, in Brooklyn," she said, crying hysterically, and all I could decipher through her tears was, "Come quick, Colin, he's in a coma!"

I rushed up the steps to Brooklyn Hospital in Fort Greene where a group of cops met me in the lobby. They told me how it had been a botched sting. Kenny had taken a position in the front leading a team of six undercover policemen into a crack house when an informer working with them turned suddenly and fired off three rounds at Kenny, hitting him in the back, *pow, pow, pow!*

I ran to Intensive Care, but a nurse blocked me, "Sorry," she said. "Only family beyond this point."

I tried to explain but I didn't have to because Rosemary, seven months pregnant, appeared and told them who I was.

The nurse backed off and Rosemary collapsed into my arms.

"Oh, Colin," she said, "Oh, oh, oh..." on and on she cried.

Several doctors joined me along with several cops to lead Rosemary back to the waiting room where her three small boys sat in shock, until they saw me. They ran to me and hugged my arms and legs and whatever else they could grab onto.

Finally, after a day and a half of phone tag I was able to get through to Ellen. She told me Pop remained curled in bed and despite her efforts to feed him, he would not eat. She told me how she had waited till after midnight to go for her run, after the throng of media outside the house had quieted down.

"But this is nothing compared to what you're dealing with," she said. "How's your brother?"

I told her how painful it was, knowing that I could have prevented this.

"Had I just said yes to Kenny when he asked me to start a security company with him none of this would have happened."

"It's not your fault," she said, but I brushed that off. I told her to go for her run at night if that worked to relax her. She said it did, and she said she was still focused on winning the Boston Marathon, more than ever, to do it for Pop.

"I want to show them," she said. "I will show them all."

I told her I was proud of her, to have a goal like that.

Bridget came to see me at the hospital three days in a row. "It's not your fault," she said, using the same words as Ellen, but that didn't settle the issue for me, or assuage my guilt.

Then one night a week later, we got some good news. A doctor came out to the waiting room and he had a smile on his face.

"We're out of the woods," he said, and Rosemary collapsed in my arms.

"Tell me," I said to the doctor.

"He's out of the coma, and he's going to make it. Do you want to see him? He's awake."

I walked behind Rosemary who ran to the room and she collapsed on the bed, hugging Kenny, as I stood in the background smiling. I watched him caress the back of her head, and it felt *so* good to see him move his hands again.

"Hey, bro! Whatcha been up to?" he said to me as I lay full

across the bed and hugged him, too.

"You had us scared there for a while," I said.

"It was only a little bullet."

"More like *three* bullets, buddy!"

"That's not enough to take me outta the game."

I felt a huge burden lift from my chest and over the next few days a sea of cops poured in and out of the room bringing Kenny their good wishes—with more than few good-natured digs as well ("Hey, your fast twitch muscles are gettin' slow in your old age").

Feeling relieved, I decided to take a walk, but as I headed out the lobby through the Emergency Room, an alarm went off and an ambulance pulled up to the dock in a rush. The back doors of the ambulance swung open and I saw a young blonde woman on a stretcher get lifted out of the back. A small boy wearing a baseball hat gripped the stretcher so tightly his fingers turned red.

"Clear the way, clear the way!" one of the doctors shouted, but as the boy ran beside the stretcher his baseball cap fell off and bounced along the ground.

In another moment the stretcher with the woman had been wheeled into an operating room, and the boy and the woman were gone. I reached down to pick up the baseball cap and handed it to the receptionist at the front desk.

"Hold this, please," I said.

"Hold it? For who?"

"For the little boy with the blonde woman."

I walked out into the quiet of the night thinking of Kenny, Ellen, Bridget, Pop—and thinking about the blonde woman and her little boy, too. I thought of all the ways the world crashes in on us unexpectedly and the imperative that creates for us to form connections with others to buffer ourselves against the blows.

CHAPTER NINETEEN

Kenny continued to make progress. By the end of the second week he was sitting up in bed, while copies of the *Daily News* piled up on a chair, all with headlines about the "Hero Cop."

He was generous. As I sat beside his bed giving him the latest on the Mets including prospects for their pitching rotation now that pitchers and catchers had reported to spring training, he did not bring up the point about the security firm, and I was grateful.

Rosemary filled the room with baked goods, which a legion of cops reduced to crumbs, and there was lots of laughter in the room, especially while the cops, along with the Mayor, poured in and out.

"Better get word to the bad guys that I'll be outta here soon and they better get on the run," Kenny joked to the Mayor, while the cops teased him that the bad guys were advertising in newspapers across the country to send reinforcements.

Each day I had a chance to catch up with Ellen, who told me she'd been making progress with Pop also, and that at least he was starting to eat soup.

"But I make him get out of bed to get the soup," she said. "I don't want any more moping around feeling sorry for himself. He said he wants to rectify things."

"Rectify?"

"I told him he and I will kick butt at Boston and that will be our way to banish the demons. We'll rectify things."

"I like it," I said, and we started making plans to see each other again.

"When do you think you can get back up here?" she said.

"In another week or so. Things should settle down by then and I will feel comfortable enough to leave Rosemary and the boys."

"Great," she said. "Can't wait to see you."

"How's your mom doing?" I said.

"Haven't talked to her."

"Come on, Ellen!"

"You can talk to her. I won't."

"Now, now! This thing wasn't her fault, and you know that," I said, but she continued to protest.

"I'll go for my run tonight and think about it."

"Yes, you do that."

"Lately, I've been able to get out earlier at night now that the vultures on the front lawn have thinned out."

"There's a kid on a bike. Wait for him to go home and that will be your all clear."

"What kid on a bike?"

"Don't worry about it. Enjoy your run!"

Later that night, I returned to the hospital after taking Kenny and Rosemary's boys back to Hicksville to get them into bed for the babysitter. I was sitting in the hospital cafeteria grabbing a sandwich when I saw the 10 o'clock news on the TV.

I wasn't paying attention until I saw a clip of Ellen running in the New York City Marathon with Nita and Turgenov and I wondered, why are they showing a clip of Ellen on the NY news?

"It's a family that has been visited by sorrow as Ellen Maloney's grandfather and trainer, Pop Gallagher, was shown to have lied about circumstances involving the first woman to run in the Boston Marathon..." I popped up to stand in front of the TV as the screen showed photos of Pop and his D.A.A. boys from 1951.

"What the..." I said, aloud.

"Now Ellen Maloney who captured this city's heart in November with her spirited run in the New York City Marathon has been visited by tragedy. Earlier this evening she was hit by a car in Boston while out for a practice run."

"Oh, my God!!!!!!!!"

"All we can say is our hearts go out to the family and we pray that she makes a speedy recovery."

"Oh, my God!" I shouted as I spun in place and my fingers fumbled with the numbers on my phone as I tried to call Ellen, but I got a voice message, "Hi, this is Ellen...."

Next, I tried Bridget, but I couldn't get through to her either, then I tried Stan.

"Yes, she was hit by a car tonight, Colin. We don't know how badly she's been hurt but I know Bridget is at the hospital, at the Carney on the Dorchester/Milton line."

I called Rosemary from a cab to tell her the news and that I would get in touch once I got to Boston.

The cab at Logan took me to the Carney and I ran into the lobby of the Emergency Room, getting there at 3 am, when a nurse stopped me.

"Wait!" she said. "You can't go any further."

"I need to see Ellen Maloney!" I said, but she put both of her big hands on my chest and pushed back against me.

"Only family allowed upstairs."

"You don't understand, I've got to see her."

"You can't go any further. Only family allowed. Her mother gave strict instructions."

"Call upstairs, talk to them!"

"We can't disturb them. The mother left instructions."

I tried to get Bridget on the phone, but no luck. I tried to argue again with the nurse, then changed to pleading, but she would not budge and she pushed me back toward the lobby where camera crews and news reporters had begun to form a pool.

Still, I tried to work my way around her, trying another corridor, but before long the nurse called security and three burly security guards led me out the doorway to the parking lot.

I tried to find a back door, and I was rushing about when I saw an ambulance driver standing against a rear wall of the building having a cigarette.

"You know how I can get into this place?"

"You here to see the girl?"

"Yes. The runner. I'm her boyfriend."

"Girl like that, I'm sure she has lots of boyfriends."

"How do I get in to see her?"

"You don't. The mother left instructions. But don't worry, she's going to be OK."

"How do you know?"

"I brought her in. It coulda been worse, but she was sitting up in the ambulance by the time we pulled up to the door of the Emergency Room."

"Thank God."

"I agree," he said, and he took a long drag on his cigarette. "Tell all her boyfriends the good news."

It started to rain as I took a cab to my apartment to get my bat, and then I took another cab to Fenway. It was raining buckets by the time I got to the ballpark and the security guard yelled at me as I banged on the front gate in the dark to let me in.

"Hey, pal, what's all the racket?"

I showed him my Press Pass. He said he didn't know what story I could possibly be doing at that hour, but nevertheless, he couldn't argue with the Press Pass. Finally, he complied and I unlatched the gate by the third base dugout and stepped out onto the clay runway in the heavy downpour.

Pound, pound, pound! I began to bang away in the rain at the clay in front of rail on the third base side where I had caught my ankle ten years earlier, and I only half noticed as the guard got on the phone and made a call asking for "someone official" at Channel 6.

Bang, bang, bang!, I continued to pound away with my bat hitting the ground hard enough to shake the sky in China on the other side of the world. Then I turned my bat on the rail, shouting out loud as I swung away, "You fucker, fucker, fucker!!!!!!!"

I have no idea how long I stood there pounding as the rain soaked me, until I heard a voice call to me from the seats near the rail, "Colin!"

It was Bridget, as the sour-faced security guard stood behind her. I could barely see her through the rain and sweat that poured off my forehead into my eyes and clogged my vision. "Go away!" I said.

"Colin, what are doing to yourself?"

"If this rail had not been here I'd be an All Star by now."

"If Pop had not been there, I'd be on a Wheaties box. Life does not come with any guarantees. Come home with me, please."

"I ran with you, Bridget, but you didn't run with me."

"What are you talking about?"

"You wouldn't let me see Ellen. You told them to keep me out."

"I didn't tell them to keep you out."

"You said 'only family' allowed."

"I was thinking of Ellen."

"You were thinking about you, Bridget. Bridget thinks only about Bridget," I said, and I began to pound away again at the rail, my bat a mass of splinters by this point.

"Stop it, Colin, please," she said, as she stepped down to the rail and reached out to grab my bat before I could take another swing. "I'm sorry. I really am."

"I wish I could hear you say that one time and believe there was real emotion behind it."

"I'm sorry if I hurt you."

I dropped my bat and I stood soaked, staring at her, my eyes trained directly at hers. "Why did you hire me, Bridget? Why did you bring me into this god damned mess?"

"So I could learn from you."

It was not the answer I expected and I didn't know what to say. Rain poured off my hair and into my eyes. It streamed under my jacket and onto my skin. I was soaked.

"You've been my teacher, Colin. You've taught me how to be a better human being."

I stopped and stared at her.

"Watching you, seeing how you feel the pain of others—knowing the depth of loss as you do—yet still you act to save others from getting hurt. You've been a powerful teacher for me, Colin. I have my lapses, as I did at the hospital, but I love you thoroughly, from my head to my toes. We all love you. Ellen, Jack and I. The Maloneys, we love you, and I hope you will give us a chance to welcome you into our family."

I stood there a long time, drenched, but I no longer felt the cold as I had. The first shoots of light broke through the clouds and the rain had stopped, I realized, as I stared at her and I saw in Bridget's eyes what I had been waiting for, true emotion.

Dawn broke behind the bleachers, as she said, "Come to the hospital with me."

I said, "Yes," as the security guard stood in the background scowling, thinking, I'm sure, about how much it was going to cost to repair the clay and repaint the rail on the third base side.

Morning light slanted across the dusky streets as Bridget drove to my apartment so I could change into dry clothes. The ambulance driver had been right. Ellen's injuries were not as severe as everyone feared. At the hospital Ellen hopped out of her bed and gave me a huge hug when I walked into her room.

"Whoa!" I said. "Careful." I led her back to her bed, as Jack and Bridget assisted, and I told her to take it easy.

"The car only clipped me," she said, showing me a bruise on her left thigh, with a railroad track line of stitches. "The doctor says it will heal quickly."

"Thank God," I said, and all was bright in the room, to match the sunshine that poured through the window, until Pop—who stood in the background by the door—said, "Can I say something?"

Slowly, everyone stopped their amiable chatter, and we turned as a group to face Pop.

"All this is my fault," he said.

Ellen was the first to respond. "No, Pop, it was an accident."

"I'm not talking about the car that hit you, Ellen. I'm talking to Bridget now."

The room went quiet, the only sound was the sound of the air conditioner as everyone stared at Pop.

"It's OK, Pop," Bridget said. "Ellen's going to be fine."

"Bridget, I owe you an apology and I want to offer that to you."

We all looked at Bridget, me especially, since I knew this was the moment she had been waiting for her whole life, and suddenly I understood "rectify."

"Yes," she said, softly. "If you want to say something to me, Pop, please do."

"I've lived with shame for what I did to you," he said. He stood in the corner, frail from having been in bed so many days, but his voice was strong as steel. "Tim Finn brought the young girl by the house after the Hyde Park race. Finn broke the rules, but, boy, could she run! We beat Semple at Hyde Park because of her. Then Finn convinced me to let her run in the Boston Marathon. Bailey was back from his injury, but Finn said if I wanted him to run on the team I had to let the girl run, too, since he had promised her, and we all know Finn is loyal."

166

"Pop, you don't have to do this," Bridget said, but he waved her off.

"I agreed to Finn's arrangement. But I had one condition. She could run Boston, as an extra on our team, but she had to wear a disguise, and she could not cross the finish line. I would bend the rules, but I would not break them.

"But I didn't know if she would keep her promise. You can never be sure, the excitement to cross the finish line when you get that close can be a strong urge.

"She was true to her word, though. She ran the race, good enough to be in the top twenty, but she stepped off the course at Commonwealth Avenue before making the turn onto Exeter Street where she might have been spotted. She found me in the lobby of the Lenox Hotel later, and I told her I was pleased with her.

"'Thank you for the chance. I did what I wanted, to be the first,' she told me.

"There was something special about her, a quality that's rare. She had integrity. I went to East Boston the next morning where they made our medals for the Marathon, and I had the man make a copy of the winner's gold medal. I paid for it myself, even though I had a row with Semple over the expense, and I called Finn to find out where the girl went to school. She was a student at Dorchester High, and I waited for her. I took her aside after school and presented her with the gold medal in the schoolyard below a tree. She looked at me with big wide eyes.

"'For me?' she said. 'A gold medal?'

"'Yes,' I told her. 'Because you did the right thing.'

"Then she got in trouble with a boy. I knew her father, old man Delaney, from Knights of Columbus, and I knew he was desperate for a solution. Mrs. Gallagher asked me if I would go over and speak to Delaney, who was about to banish the girl, his youngest daughter. 'Don't do anything if the girl doesn't want our help,' Mrs. Gallagher said, but I knew Mrs. Gallagher wanted a girl, more than anything.

I had spent my whole life with my boys, and Mrs. Gallagher had no one. We couldn't have children, and she blamed me, I felt, though she would never say anything. That's what gave me the idea that if I could bring home a little girl it would ease the burden for me with Mrs. Gallagher.

"I went to Delaney's that night. He was the talk of the firehouse that his daughter had gotten in trouble, and he was pleased that I offered to take his problem away.

"You were tiny, just six weeks old, and your mother's sisters supported her to keep her baby, if that's what she wanted. But old man Delaney had made up his mind. The baby was going, and the girl was going next. He had made plans to send her to a convent like her elder sister Josephine, and I think after all that happened, he decided to send the other one, Delia, to a convent, too.

"So I took you that night, before old man Delaney could change his mind, and we agreed to do the paperwork later. But what I did next has been my great shame, and I could not have expected you to forgive me if I had ever told you this to your face.

"I walked out of the house with you, but as I held you wrapped in a blanket, I saw a door open in back. It was your mother coming around from the back of the house, and she met me on the sidewalk out front. She stood between the house and the corner, looking at me in the dark with the same determined eyes she had trained on me the day she had finished the marathon, but now she expected integrity from me as I had expected it from her.

"'Please,' she said. 'I want to keep my baby.'

"'But your father,' I said.

"She shook her head, crying, 'I want to keep my baby,' she said, blocking me, her face swollen with tears, as we stood in the light of a lone streetlamp. 'Please don't take my baby away.'

"She was thin and frail, hardly the lean, wiry figure who had finished the marathon, but as I looked into her eyes, so pained, I could see Mrs. Gallagher at home preparing the crib, and I knew

I had only to make it past her, get around her, just three more feet, and Mrs. Gallagher would have what she had always wanted and I would be free to spend time with my boys.

"'Please?' the girl said again. Then she said the words I have never been able to put out of my mind, no matter how many times I have walked to the shore at Castle Island and stared out at the sea.

"'Please do the right thing,' she said.

"I looked past her to the corner, and I answered with words I have regretted my whole life, 'Your mistake is not my problem,' I said.

"And so, Bridget, I made you pay for what I did that night. Your whole life you have been a reminder to me of how weak I am. I deprived you of a mother and a life with her and I have deprived you of accomplishments at every turn. I have blocked you, Bridget, so I would not have to consider what I had done to you. I did not give you the support you deserved because I never deserved you in the first place. I was foolish. No man can hold back the sea, nor the flood of emotions that I have held back for so long, trying to forget how I took your life from you. But I tried to make things right with Ellen. I want you to know that. I tried to do right by Ellen, training her and offering her encouragement, so she might have what I denied you. But in the end, as time whittles down, what I really want to do is do right by you. But I don't know how to do that, Bridget, except to say…" and he paused as the air conditioner made the only sound.

"I'm sorry."

CHAPTER TWENTY

Reporters jammed the hospital lobby swarming around Ellen when the hospital released her the next morning.

"Ellen, are you going to run Boston?" Several called in unison.

Jack answered for her. "We have six weeks to go before the marathon. We'll let the doctors decide if she'll be ready to go by the third Monday in April."

"How are you feeling?" several asked.

"The car that hit me stopped rather than ran off," she said with a big smile. "So I'm making progress with my accidents. I'm feeling fine. Thank you."

"What about Pop's lie?" Steele asked as he moved to the fore with a cameraman and thrust a microphone toward Ellen.

Jack moved between Ellen and Steele with fire in his eyes.

"Why don't you go f..." he said, but he caught himself before finishing the sentence, as Bridget squeezed his arm. The family continued to push through the front door and in another moment they were outside and in the car—Ellen, Bridget, Jack and Pop—and off they went.

I stayed behind to collect Ellen's things, when I saw Tim Finn. He was sitting in the coffee shop behind the lobby in his jean jacket with his gray ponytail under a baseball cap. He waved to me by raising his cup.

I waited to make sure all the news reporters were gone, including

Steele, then I went in and sat down across from him.

"Thank God it was only a superficial wound," he said.

"She wants to run Boston. But the doctors will make that call. She has a big bruise on the side of her left leg."

"She'll run. She comes from tough stock."

"That she does."

"Speaking of lineage, Bridget's mother wants to see her."

I looked at Finn, and leaned forward. "Tell me."

"I'll introduce you to someone who can give you the answers."

I nodded, OK. "Where?"

"Take your car, follow me. There's a Brigham's on River Street, next to Osco's. She's waiting for us there."

I did not need an introduction, since I recognized the gray-haired lady from the school cafeteria.

"Colin, meet Delia Delaney," Tim Finn said, as we joined the tall, broad-shouldered woman in a booth at the back of the ice cream shop.

"Hello, again," I said, smiling, and I extended my hand. She had a firm grip and she was all business as she jumped right into her story.

"Margaret's with me. She's been here since October. She was living in St. Louis when she contacted me. She said she wanted to see Bridget, her child, while she still had time."

"Time? What do you mean?"

"Margaret has lung cancer. She doesn't know how much more time she has." She paused before continuing. "I was shocked. I didn't even know Margaret was alive after the attack in El Salvador."

"None of us did," Tim said to me.

"What happened?"

"She was Mother Superior at her mission in El Salvador in the 70's. You knew that, right?" Delia said.

"Yes."

"The army didn't like her putting herself in the middle of their fight against the rebels, saving their enemies' babies, and so they made Margaret their enemy too. One day a rogue group from the army attacked her mission and killed four nuns they suspected were arranging the adoptions. It was big news. Margaret was listed as one of the four killed, but they burned the building and we never had a burial for Margaret."

"I don't understand. How did she survive?"

"We don't know," Delia said. "But she did. She was late to a meeting at the convent, or something like that. In any case, the US government was eager to keep her survival secret, too. They knew certain generals would want to try again, especially if they thought there was a possibility Margaret could testify against them in a world court on war crimes. Killing four nuns, the world pays attention to something like that."

"I'm sure."

"So State put the DEA on it, since the rogue generals making mayhem were involved in drugs, too. The DEA set Margaret up in St. Louis with a new identity to protect her. She became a school principal for her career. I only learned all this when she called me last fall to ask if she could come to Boston and stay with me while she reconnected with Bridget."

"You let her come?"

"Yes. She watches Bridget on TV every night and she watches Ellen, too. Often she'll go to the practice field in Hyde Park where Ellen trains and sit in the stands to watch her."

"Then things got hot," said Tim.

"Hot?"

"The Runner in Red story," said Delia. "Bridget was getting close to solving that, and that raised a red flag with the DEA. They know all about Margaret's background, how she was the first woman to run a marathon in America, but they needed to keep the story alive that she was dead in order to continue to protect her."

"Explain."

"Some of the generals who planned the attack on her convent are still active. They're part of a new drug ring down there that's quite lucrative for them. The last thing they need is to have Margaret alive to testify against them. You can imagine how that crowd would lose if people found out that a nun they tried to kill in 1979 for protecting babies is still alive."

"Wow," I said.

"That's why Clinton wants to get her out of Boston."

"Clinton?"

"He's the head of the DEA in this region these days, the guy who oversees the operation against the rogue generals and the drug cartel."

"I know Clinton. I met him once."

"He's upset that his team in St. Louis let Margaret give them the slip. He didn't know she was in Boston, but he came to me after you visited our school and put a camera in Margaret's face."

"*Our* school?"

"That day you came to the Washington Irving Middle School. I went out the back door, but you went upstairs and put a camera in Margaret's face."

"Margaret? She works at the school?"

"She was the principal, until Clinton and the DEA took her undercover again."

"The lady who told me 'All my children are special to me.' That was Margaret, Bridget's mother?"

"Our regular principal suddenly took medical leave in October. Downtown needed somebody to fill in fast. Because Margaret had years of experience in St. Louis I was able to get her into that job. It was good for her, since it gave her a chance to work with children again."

"I was face to face with Margaret?"

"Yes, and that made Clinton nervous that a TV station had her on tape, showing her as alive as can be. That's not something the DEA wants the rogue generals in El Salvador to know about."

I didn't know what to say, and I looked at Finn.

"It's complicated," he said.

"You think?!?"

"But that's only half of it," said Delia. "That's Clinton's motivation for protecting Margaret. She doesn't care a whit about her own safety. If you knew Margaret, you'd understand that. But Clinton convinced her that if it ever became known she was alive, the forces that hurt the children when she was the Mother Superior might start a whole new round of carnage to pressure her to keep quiet. That's what Margaret cares about, the impact this could have on others, and that's why she's willing to do what Clinton says, to keep others from getting hurt."

A tee-ball team of little girls in blue Dorchester Plumbing t-shirts poured in for ice cream following their game. We let them order and make their noise, then we picked up once it was quiet again.

"What do you want me to do?" I said.

"We don't have much time," Delia said. "Clinton wants to fly her out tonight. He wants to get her back to St. Louis. Then he plans to change her identity again and move her to a new city. Start all over again to keep the story going that she's dead."

"She leaves tonight?"

"Clinton has her booked on a flight at 8 pm. But he agreed to let her have a meeting at the gate with Bridget before they board. A short meeting, but it will give Margaret the chance she's been waiting for her whole life and I'm sure Bridget would love that, too, to meet her mother."

"Can you be the middleman?" Tim Finn asked me.

"Sure," I said without hesitation, but I had one more question, this one for Finn. "Tim, are you Bridget's father?"

"No, her uncle."

174

He had a photo in his wallet of the 1951 D.A.A. championship team. He tapped the image of a tall, crew cut blonde fellow standing next to him in the picture. "That's Ben, my brother. He took a fancy to Margaret after her gutsy run in the '51 Boston Marathon."

"Where's Ben now?"

"Cambodia, May, 1970. He was a Marine Colonel when his chopper went down with our other brother from the running team, Jimmy."

"She'll be proud to know that her father was brave," Delia said.

I paused to absorb the fact of that loss, then I said, "I don't get it. A simple thing like a girl gets pregnant, and so many lives get damaged."

"Margaret was mortified," Delia said. "You have no idea how angry Poppa was with her."

"Still, I don't get it. All the lives that have been damaged or destroyed."

"The power of shame," Tim said. "It was a different time, a world long gone."

"What do you need me to do?" I said.

Before I got to the TV station I called Stan and asked him to get the out-takes from the video I had shot at the school in Dorchester.

"We don't usually keep tape for stories we don't do. I can't promise you your tape is still around," he said.

I asked him to do his best and I told him to meet me in the parking lot with the Beta cassette if he could find it. "And order me a truck."

"A truck?"

"A truck with a monitor where I can play the tape, but make sure the tape you give me is the only copy. Sorry if I'm being cryptic, but call Bridget, too, and ask her to meet me in the parking lot ASAP."

"These are cryptic times," he said, and I understood all over again why Bridget valued his friendship so much.

"What's going on?" Bridget said, as she slid in on the passenger side of the truck which I had parked behind the maintenance garage.

"Anybody see you?"

"No, what's up?"

"You remember this," I said, and I popped in the cassette from Stan, which he had found. It showed the footage I had shot at the Washington Irving the day we had gone looking for Delia Delaney.

"Yes. But we didn't do that story. We did the girls in track shoes."

"Good thing we didn't do the story. Otherwise, we would have exposed your mother to real danger."

She looked at me crookedly. "What's going on, Colin?"

"That's your mother," I said, and I pointed to the monitor and the shot of the elderly woman in the floral dress who covered her face and started crying as I peppered her with questions.

I could see Bridget gasp, and she sat back in her seat. Then she leaned in close to the monitor and stared at the woman with the deep blue eyes. "That's Margaret?"

"Yes, we were close that day. But you're going to get another chance."

She looked at me, crookedly again, and I told her about my meeting with Tim Finn and Delia.

"Delia said Margaret wants to see you at the airport tonight, but you have to promise me one thing, Bridget."

She nodded. "What?"

"You have to promise me you won't do anything to compromise her. She's in danger, and you can't do anything that might reveal who she is."

"I promise."

"You gotta promise me, Bridget!"

"I promise," she said, and she looked at her watch. "It's 6:30. Let's get to the airport. We can take my car."

"One thing I gotta do first," I said, and I removed the tape from the cassette player. I pulled the tape out in a long string, destroying it.

"Now we can go," I said.

The line to pass through screening at Logan International Airport on that busy Saturday night looked like the finish line of a marathon. The crowd jammed the three metal detectors leading to the American Airlines gates like clogged shoots at the end of a race.

Jack, Ellen, and Pop came from the other direction as we arrived. They had been at Pop's house when Bridget called inviting them to share the special moment with her.

"How much time we got?" Bridget said to me.

"There's half an hour before they close the doors. We're good," I said, and I waved to Jack, Ellen, and Pop to follow us.

We got through screening and ran to Gate 32 at the end of the concourse, where I saw Clinton standing with a large group of elderly men and women. The group had a banner, "St Louis Garden Club," which served as the rally point for the group to gather around before their flight.

"St. Louis, Flight 67, boarding at Gate 32," came the call over the PA.

Smart of Clinton, I thought, to hide Margaret among a group of elderly Garden Club passengers going to the same destination. Many of the ladies had blue hair and the men were mostly paunchy and bald. I scanned the crowd for Margaret and I saw her standing behind Clinton. She blended in perfectly in her brown coat and gray wool knit hat. I looked at Bridget, who was scanning the group. I watched her eyes, filled as they were with anticipation to be this close, feet away from the person who would provide the missing element in her life, the woman whose face—once she saw it—would fill a hole she had carried for a lifetime.

Then she saw her!

Bridget's eyes opened wide as she found Margaret's eyes in the Garden Club crowd and Margaret found hers. They locked in on each other and smiled, at the same moment there came a commotion in the corridor behind us leading to the gate.

"Hold the flight!" Steele said as he came running with a cameraman. Behind him, Roman and Junior came running, too.

"Oh, Christ!" I heard Clinton say.

I saw Bridget take a step toward Margaret, and I stepped in front of her to block her.

"No," I said.

"I must."

"You promised!"

She looked into my eyes. "This is my mother, Colin. I need to touch her."

"Touch her and you'll leave a hole where your soul used to be," I said, as Steele and his cameraman ran up to us. Steele ordered his man to point the camera at Bridget and pull in tight on her eyes.

"Bridget, who's your mother?" Steele said, as Bridget continued to stare at me, pleading almost.

At the gate Clinton worked quickly with the gate agent to gather the Garden Club crowd and board them.

Bridget glanced at me one last time, then took a step toward the group as Clinton waved his arms like a pinwheel to corral the elderly travelers. He moved them swiftly toward the airplane door as Steele directed his cameraman to follow Bridget.

"Follow her eyes," he said. "Stay on her eyes!"

Bridget looked to the side to avoid looking at Margaret, and Margaret did the same, except for one brief moment when their eyes connected, and I saw the pain and longing and loss in both their expressions.

"Who's your mother, Bridget?" Steele said. "Show us the Runner in Red!"

Bridget walked quickly now toward the group, and she waded into the middle of two dozen elderly men and women as Steele and his cameraman followed. Then she lunged forward and hugged a severe-looking, broad-shouldered woman in a red coat and said, "Mom!"

Steele and his cameraman were all over the woman, whose husband, a tiny man in a leisure suit, tried to intercede, saying, "Hey, hey, hey!"

"Margaret Delaney, tell us about your marathon run," Steele said to the woman in the red coat as her husband edged in to block him, but Steele's cameraman pushed even harder and the poor man went flying back and skidded along the carpet on the seat of his pants.

Clinton worked fast with the gate agent to get the rest of the group, including Margaret, onto the plane. As she walked down the jetway, she turned to look back one last time, and she and Bridget met eyes again, and I could see tears in both their eyes.

Finally, the lady in the red coat and her husband were separated from Steele and his cameraman and the gate agent showed Steele that he had the wrong person.

"These are the Carvers," the agent said, thrusting two boarding passes under Steele's nose. "Mr. and Mrs. Russell Carver."

Soon the plane was boarded, including the Carvers who huffed and puffed and threatened lawsuits, and soon the plane pulled from the gate. It rolled along the taxiway to take off as Steele dusted the dirt off his jacket and Roman walked over to Bridget.

"Nice move," he said, a model of composure. "But *so* dumb."

"No, the right thing."

"We could have lined up exclusive rights and made a mint. But some people are wedded to their old fashioned values."

The roundhouse punch Jack threw came out of the blue and though Jack pulled his punch at the last moment and did not strike Roman, still Roman staggered backwards and bounced against a wall, mussing his well-coifed hair, as his knees buckled.

"Some people are wedded to their over-inflated egos. But not enough for me to waste the skin off my knuckles," Jack said.

Bridget smiled as Roman stood up straight again, smoothing his lapels. Then Jack took Bridget's hand and the three of them—Bridget, Ellen, and Jack—walked to the tall broad window overlooking the runway and watched the plane to St. Louis speed away and lift off in the dark.

"I'm proud of you, Mom," Ellen said after a long moment, and Bridget hugged her, with tears in her eyes.

"There are two times I wished you were mine," Pop said. "The day you faced off against me at the finish line, and tonight, seeing what you did just now."

"Can we be friends?" Bridget said.

He reached out his hand to her, and she took it.

"I'm sorry," she said.

Ellen sped around the track at Hyde Park High in the slanting light of the warm spring afternoon, as Pop kept the watch and Jack and Bridget leaned in for a look at her time.

"How's she doing?" Jack said.

"Damn fast," said Pop. "Good as she's ever been."

"Two weeks to go till Boston. We'll let the docs know about this. See if they'll give her a green light."

"I don't see why they wouldn't," said Pop.

I watched Bridget watch Ellen reduce her pace to a jog after her series of fast interval mile runs and I could see the thousand mile stare in Bridget's eye, mixed with intense pride. I could only guess

what she might be thinking. *Like mother, like daughter*, maybe?
It was Pop who broke the spell. "Why don't you go to her?"
She looked at him, puzzled.
"She's doing her cool down run. She needs company."
Bridget kicked off her dove gray Ferragamo shoes and, barefoot, took off across the infield grass to catch Ellen on the far straightaway. Ellen saw her coming and opened her arms to hug her mom, and the two of them jogged together, their laughter carrying back across the infield grass to us.
"How do you do it?" I asked Jack who stared at his two ladies with a faraway gaze.
"Do what?"
"Your whole life you've let yourself be dangled in the middle between the two of them? How do you stay sane, man?"
He smiled a broad Irish grin.
"I don't think of it as 'dangled,' son." He paused to watch Bridget and Ellen continue their run together. "I'm not a scholar, but the Jesuits had me at Boston College and there's one thing I remember from my 8 am classes after a long night bending the elbow at the Tam. Dostoevsky said 'Hell is the absence of love.' Maybe that's what love is, embracing the dangling. And you're OK with that, the loss of control, because that's what it takes to meet the other person's need. Who knows, what do you think, Pop?"
I looked at Pop, who nodded.
My mom was right. We all have diamonds inside us, waiting for us to discover them. We muck our diamonds up over a lifetime, that's for sure, but we can uncake them if we choose to make ourselves vulnerable.

CHAPTER TWENTY-ONE

B y all measures, the 2000 marathon was one of the most successful Boston Marathons ever, largely for the attention paid to women runners and their achievements.

Nearly all the exhibits at the Marathon Expo at the Hynes Auditorium that weekend celebrating a new century for the marathon carried tributes to the women who had blazed the way for the thousands of women runners entered in that year's contest.

Women champions, from Uta Pippig in the 90s, to Ingrid Kristiansen, Joan Benoit and Allison Roe in the 80s, to the stars of the 70s, including Gayle Barron, Miki Gorman, and Kim Merritt. They, along with the earliest pioneers, Sara Mae Berman, Roberta Gibb and Kathrine Switzer, signed autographs in booths up and down the packed aisles which featured exhibits showcasing the latest in shoes, clothing, and dietary supplements.

One of the most popular events, and most heavily attended, was a panel discussion organized by Gloria Ratti, VP of the Boston Athletic Association, featuring the "women pioneers," as they were billed. This was the group most directly involved in the struggle with Jock and Pop, including not only Bridget, who served as moderator, but Switzer, Berman, Gibb, and several of the early winners, Nina Kuscsik and Jackie Hansen.

"Why?" asked a young man in the audience during the Q and A. "Why did it take so long for women to be given a chance?"

The panelists looked at Bridget, and several said, "Do you want to handle that?"

"Because men were afraid of us, though they had nothing to fear," Bridget said. "Beyond that I don't have the foggiest."

The panel discussion concluded with a video presentation offered by Guy Morse, B.A.A. director, showcasing the history of women's running at Boston. Regarding the Runner in Red, the film acknowledged the long-standing legend that there had been a female runner in 1951—the graphic showed Freddie Norman's photo of the hooded figure climbing Heartbreak Hill—while the narrator intoned, "It is believed that a woman in a red hood ran the race in 1951 before women were permitted to compete, and it's been contended that the woman may have been Margaret Delaney, mother of Bridget Maloney, a champion from the 1970s. But doubt remains since Margaret Delaney has never been found and the story has never been authenticated. Thus the 'Runner in Red' remains an urban legend and an unsolved mystery today."

Questioned by young girls in the audience, Bridget acknowledged the likelihood that the legend was true, but concluded by saying, "I've never met my mother."

A male reporter tried to push the point, "Do you know if anyone ever found her?" but Bridget said, "People are still looking, I'm sure," and the discussion turned to modern topics involving women runners, including the accomplishments of African women, especially the Kenyans. Then questions were raised for the panelists about diets they had employed while training, and just like that, after all the struggle and heartbreak, the issue faded, like the dew on leaves as the sun rises.

I thought of Roman who had failed to get what he wanted on so many levels, and I was happy to see the Maloneys become a functioning family again. As they gathered—Bridget, Jack, and Ellen—I went outside for a walk to collect my thoughts.

Boylston Street, the busy Boston thoroughfare in front of the Hynes, hummed as workers hammered snow fencing into place to create the race's final long straightaway. Pedestrians ambled about without cars to impede them, while runners from around the world in colorful sweats created sinewy paths through the assembly under a blue sky. I merged with the crowd, permitting myself to be borne along until I came to a spot in front of the Prudential Building that had served as the race's finish line until the mid-1980s.

That's when the John Hancock organization assumed sponsorship of the race and moved the finish line to the place in front of the Public Library where Ellen and I had convened one night.

With my toe, I edged back three feet from the spot in the road in front of the Prudential where the tape had stretched in 1971, a spot long since erased, and I found the place in the street where Pop had blocked Bridget.

I saw him in my mind's eye, arms flailing, and I saw Bridget— "chest rising and falling, hair matted, exhausted after coming all that way," as news accounts had described it—and I felt the electricity of that moment, undiminished by the years.

I felt the emotion that had marked their relationship and had driven Pop and Bridget apart, a misunderstanding of intentions that had poisoned Pop's life and had soured Bridget's, until she found it in herself to save herself from bitterness, pride, and regrets.

And that she did! She had let Margaret go, giving up a chance to touch her, and thus she had disproved those who said, "Bridget thinks only about Bridget."

It was an oldies song about miracles by Jefferson Starship that had made me think of Bridget that day in the storefront. I had answered her call and followed her, and she had offered me a miracle. She changed my life. And so it was that another song came to mind as I stood on Boylston Street, running my toe along the abandoned finish line, three feet short of the spot where Bridget might have gained a world record: "You Can't Always Get What You Want."

I thought an additional line should be added to the song for Bridget: "But sometimes you get paid back for doing good."

The next day at the Boston Marathon Bridget got something back for sublimating her need to meet the greater need of another.

We dropped Ellen off at the start at Hopkinton on Monday, race day. Doctors cleared her to run, and she was eager though she knew in her heart—and we knew as well—that her accident had cost her valuable training time and she might be missing her edge.

But we did not talk about that, and we drove to Newton after dropping her off at the start, where we found a spot under the big oak tree on Heartbreak Hill where Freddie Norman had spotted Margaret running with Tim Finn. We carved out a place for ourselves, Jack, Bridget and me, to watch the race and be ready to cheer for Ellen when she passed on her way up Heartbreak Hill.

The radio captured the crack of the starting gun as it sounded at noon in Hopkinton under a blue, unmarred sky seventeen miles away. People of all ages and sizes lined Commonwealth Avenue in Newton, creating a corridor, waiting for the leaders and the legions of runners yet to come.

"Hey!" a man called to Bridget as he passed. He recognized her and she smiled, but for the most part spectators were focused on their needs, which included finding Sammy or Susie, checking to see who had the picnic basket or most importantly, finding a good spot to watch and wait, and as such we moved about in relative anonymity.

I was the first to spot the dark sedan as it pulled to the curb across the street. Through an opening in the crowd, I saw a woman, long and reed-like, get out of the back. She wore a red scarf and navy coat, but it was her blue eyes, set wide in her wrinkled face that attracted my attention, and I saw a man in a jean jacket with a gray ponytail, Tim Finn, get out of the car on the other side.

He took the woman by the hand, and he pointed toward us. I

looked at Bridget, who chatted amiably with an elderly man who told her he had watched her in 1971 "speed by like the wind," and she thanked him. Then she called to Jack who was not listening because he was focused on the woman in the navy coat and red scarf as she walked toward us, and at that moment I realized Jack was in cahoots with Tim Finn.

Margaret Delaney came walking tenuously, picking her way left then right through the crowd, and when she reached a point directly across the street from us, she stood facing Bridget, who turned.

Suddenly the chasm that had separated mother and daughter through time and space had been compressed to twenty feet, and I saw a tear appear in Margaret Delaney's eye as their eyes met.

Spectators crossed Commonwealth Ave. back and forth in advance of the runners yet to come, and Jack stepped into the street with them. He took Margaret's arm on one side as Tim Finn took her other arm, and they led her to her daughter.

The two stood face-to-face, mother and daughter, before either of them spoke. Then Margaret ran a finger along Bridget's check, as Bridget closed her eyes, and when she opened them she was crying.

"Dearest," Margaret said.

"Mom," Bridget said, and she hugged her mother.

"He made it possible," Margaret said, and she gestured back across the street to the sedan where the Governor sat in the passenger's seat with the darkened window half rolled up. "Your uncle talked to Mr. Clinton."

The Governor saluted with a finger to his forehead, but he remained in the car so as not to call attention to himself.

"Do you have to leave again?" Bridget said. "Can you stay?"

Margaret shook her head. "I promised Mr. Clinton I would return tonight. He wants to start his process with me all over again."

"Why does it have to be this way?"

"Those with harmful intent might take out their anger on anyone

I touch. The children in that poor, suffering country. Maybe even on you, or Ellen. I can't take that chance."

"And so this is your choice?"

"Yes, it is the right thing."

"You're happy with that choice?"

"No, but it is the right thing to do."

"Will I ever see you again?"

Margaret smiled, a thin smile. "This is our moment, small as it is."

"I have so much I want to ask you."

"And I have so much to tell."

"I have waited for this moment longer than you can know."

"As have I. Our lives spin away from us, beyond our control, once we step from our prescribed paths."

Bridget touched Margaret's arm, as if to reassure herself that her mother was real. "Do you remember this place, nearly fifty years ago?"

Margaret turned to look at the street. The soft breeze buffeted her red scarf and she smiled. "I do. I remember everything about it. Which is why I brought you something." She reached into her coat and removed a felt cloth, which she opened to reveal a diamond. "I have kept this for you, waiting for this moment, if I ever had the chance."

"What's this?" Bridget said.

"It's the diamond, from the medal Pop gave me in 1951. I removed it after you were born. I gave the medal to your mother, Pop's wife, to keep for you. But I kept the diamond so I would have something for myself."

"You kept this, all these years?"

"Yes, a link to you. But now it's for Ellen, so the three of us can be connected. Will you give it to Ellen for me?"

"Why does it have to be like this?" Bridget said, as she wrapped the diamond in the felt and put it into her pocket.

"We can't control what happens to us. We can only control our response."

"Can you stay long enough to see her pass?"

"I told Mr. Clinton that was my requirement."

Bridget smiled, and it wasn't too long before a huge buzz rose from the crowd signaling that the first men were about to arrive.

Four of them—two Kenyans, a Mexican and an Ethiopian—sped by in a blur and the crowd cheered.

"Where is she, Jack?" said Bridget, and Jack turned up the volume on his radio so we all could hear the report from Kathrine Switzer.

Kathrine, riding in the cab of a motorcycle covering the women's race, said, "The women leaders, Nita and Turgenov, have just turned off Route 16 onto Commonwealth Ave. and have begun their climb up Heartbreak Hill. Behind them a pack of a dozen women, including hometown hero Ellen Maloney, trail by a quarter of a mile. But now, wait, three women, two Kenyans and a Japanese runner, have moved out of that pack and have started to chase the two leaders."

"Where's Ellen?" I asked Bridget, but Kathrine answered the question.

"Ellen Maloney did not make a move with the three who just broke away. She is hanging back, much as she did at New York, but there has to be some concern that the injury she sustained when she was hit by a car six weeks ago is becoming a factor."

Several minutes later Nita and Turgenov (with Kathrine in a motorcycle sidecar beside them) sped by as the crowd cheered. They were followed by the three women who had broken from the pack, running in a tight knot.

Soon a large roar rose from the crowd and we did not need the radio to know that Ellen was coming!

Arms shot into the air all along the curb where spectators stood ten deep and cheered for Ellen, the hometown hero. Margaret stood next to Bridget, her hands cupped over her mouth in awe as Ellen passed.

Blonde ponytail flapping, she wore red shorts and to our surprise she must have found Pop's treasure chest because she was wearing Tim Finn's yellow D.A.A. singlet from the 1951 race for a top. As she climbed Heartbreak Hill in a pack with half a dozen other women she looked for us under the tall oak, as we had planned, and she broke out in a broad smile as she picked Bridget, Jack and me out of the crowd.

But her brow knit at the sight of the elderly woman in the red scarf, until suddenly she realized, and she broke into a grin as Bridget and Margaret blew kisses.

After she was gone I stared a long moment at the tall oak, and I looked at Margaret who stood in front of this tree again where nearly half a century earlier Freddie Norman's wife had snapped her photo. I marveled at all of it, the rhythms of life, how everything fits together—three generations united—and in the end things make sense.

Tim Finn tapped Margaret's shoulder, signaling it was time to go, but Bridget held her hand and looked into her mother's eyes.

"Why did you stop that day?"

"Those were the rules," Margaret said.

"You were the first woman. The world would have given you the credit."

"We did not break the rules."

"But the rules were not fair."

"No, but they were the rules and we were governed by them."

"Why didn't you break that one rule, one time?"

"Why didn't I keep you?" she said, and again Tim tapped Margaret, time to go.

"Thank you," Bridget said, as her eyes filled. "For coming."

"This will be my memory. My special memory above all others."

Margaret hugged Bridget, but Bridget took her hand one last time. "Clinton can hide you. But tell him, I will find you again."

Margaret smiled. "I would not expect less from my fiercely competitive daughter."

They hugged, then Tim led her across the street to the Governor's car. She didn't turn again until she was in the car and it was rolling away. Then her hand rose to the glass and she touched the window for one last shared moment.

Slowly the car turned the corner and Margaret melted into the crowd again as she had done on this road nearly fifty years earlier.

Another motorcycle with a side-car passed, and the reporter, Uta Pippig, craned her neck as if looking for someone, then I realized: she was looking for us.

A three-time winner of the Boston Marathon from 1993 to 1995, Uta Pippig had been tapped by a TV station, not Channel 6, to follow Ellen and report on "Boston's Comeback Gal" for a local audience.

She gestured to Bridget and me to get into the cab. The cameraman had been cued on his role because he handed me his camera and stepped out of the sidecar, which had room only for Uta, Bridget and me.

I caught on quick that my role would be to film the race the rest of the way, and off we went in pursuit of Ellen, as Jack waved goodbye then ran to his car to drive to the finish.

By the time we caught up to Ellen she was cresting Heartbreak Hill near Boston College. Students jamming the street recognized her as an alum, and they went crazy.

Steadily, she gained on two of the three who had broken away, one of the Kenyans and the Japanese runner. The two ran shoulder to shoulder as Ellen pulled in behind them at Boston College, then on the downhill beyond the college Ellen passed the two as if they were standing still.

"Oh, boy, she means business!" Uta said. Then she turned up the volume on her radio to get Kathrine's report and we learned that the other Kenyan from the break-away group—a twenty-year-old named Jema Kipyat making her marathon debut—had pulled behind Nita and Turgenov as the two leaders approached Cleveland Circle, the 23-mile mark.

Ellen dropped in a 5:07 mile, prompting Uta to say, *"That* was fast!" and the effort pulled Ellen close enough to Nita and Turgenov on Beacon Street that we could see their backs. By Coolidge Corner, the 24-mile mark, Ellen was closing in on Nita and Turgenov as we rode in the motorcycle sidecar beside her.

On the radio, Kathrine reported that Kipyat had passed the two favorites and was now running all by herself with a 50-yard lead heading into Kenmore Square.

In Kenmore Square, below the Citgo sign and the 25-mile mark, Ellen pulled even with Nita and Turgenov and wasted little time taking them on. She passed them in a rush as she approached the Storrow Drive overpass with less than a mile to go, and yes, she *was* all about business.

That's when I saw red on her leg. I did not see it right away because it blended with her red shorts, but clearly the area of her stitches had begun to bleed. I glanced at Bridget who saw the bleeding, too, and she looked at me with great concern.

I motioned to Ellen, mouthing "Your leg, your leg," as our motorcycle pulled close to her, but she shook her head, blowing me off, and gave me a look like, "So what!"

She was on a mission, and she strode hard to catch Kipyat, a young woman the same age she had been when she had tried for the Olympics. She pulled even with Kipyat as the two entered the underpass below the Mass. Ave. bridge.

When they came out the other side, Kathrine had spotted the blood because she was talking about it on the radio and her cameraman put a close-up of Ellen's left leg on the TV, which was carried on

191

the big screen at the corner of Commonwealth Ave. and Hereford Street. The shot of her bleeding leg looked two stories tall on the big screen, causing the huge crowd to gasp.

I saw the determined look in Ellen's eye as we pulled even with her again, and I focused my camera in tight on her for a close-up. I read her lips, and she said with a smile, as if talking to me directly, "Step up! Step up!" Then striding hard, she turned onto Hereford Street and the stretch before the last turn and the final straightaway as we rode in the motorcycle sidecar beside her.

Now all her concentration was straight ahead on Kipyat, who she passed as she made the turn from Hereford Street onto Boylston, and the sound from the crowd lining the final straightaway was like a volcanic eruption.

Beaming, she came striding fast down the final straightaway in the lead, and the crowd roared. This was the stretch I had pedaled along that night with Ellen while she ran beside me and had talked about "getting it done."

Spectators on both sides of Boylston Street replicated a "wave" from a baseball game. They threw their hands into the air cheering in sync with Ellen's smooth stride as she powered up Boylston to the finish in her red shorts and yellow D.A.A. singlet, expanding her lead, and cameras on the media bridge showed her approach on the big screens as millions more watched on TV.

Then with a block to go, she did something impromptu: she thrust her right arm into the air and shouted, "For Pop! For Pop!"

The crowd matched her with a chant of, "For Pop! For Pop!" as Bridget, sitting beside me in the motorcycle sidecar, beamed. Pop stood on the bridge above the finish line, also smiling broadly, and the cameras projected his proud face onto the big screens.

And that's how the race ended, with Ellen punching a hole in the blue, cloudless sky with her fist as she crossed the finish line, shouting, "For Pop! For Pop!"

And with that, she banished the demons!

The Last 385 Yards

During the celebration at the finish line, Bridget gave me Margaret's diamond to give to Ellen. At Fenway she had invited me to join the Maloney family, now the gift of Margaret's diamond was the formal expression of that.

I had the diamond set into an engagement ring and I took Ellen to a resort on Cape Cod that summer to ask her to marry me.

She said yes, and we walked along the shore at sunset. I held her hand, the one with the ring, and gently I squeezed her fingertips, savoring the envelopment. Everything had come together to bring us to this point, all the roads beginning with our chance encounter on a path in Philadelphia had coalesced to deliver us to this place where the sun-splashed sky met the open sea and created a path to a new life.

All life came from the sea, as Pop knew, life as brutal as those who threatened Margaret's war-torn children, yet life as graceful as the curl of Ellen's fingertips. Like the waves that lapped unevenly at the shoreline, however, there was nothing even about life or predictable about the way alternately it visits sadness upon us, or offers hope.

And that is how it was when Bridget found Margaret again.

Bridget had told Margaret she would not stop searching for her, and she did not. She learned that Clinton had created a new life for Margaret in Seattle, but it was not to be a long life. That was the sadness in Bridget's discovery: she learned that Margaret's lung cancer had progressed rapidly after their meeting at the Boston Marathon in April.

Bridget convinced Clinton to let her come to Seattle, and that's where hope comes in. Bridget was able to be at Margaret's bedside for her passing, and in the end mother and daughter were reunited.

Bridget gave Margaret what she wanted, which was to remain undiscovered so no children in Central America would be put in jeopardy. In return Bridget got what she wanted. As she held her mother's hand and Margaret took her last breath, Bridget got to experience where she came from. She came from someone special who acted for others, a lady who embraced her vulnerability; thus Bridget gained the connection she had sought so avidly. She no longer had to feel isolated. Now she could value herself and that gave her a platform to connect to others, which is what she had told me in the car after visiting Sister Josephine she wanted most: connection.

That was the lesson I learned during my journey with Bridget, that we get when we give.

As Ellen and I walked along the shore, kicking at the surf, I looked down and I focused again on how the waves did not roll evenly below our feet. Instead, they rushed up the incline in staccato fashion, making white, foamy edges as they slipped back and tried to come up the slope again.

Life contains sadness—the philosopher Hobbes described life as "short, brutish and mean"— but it's climbing up the inclines of adversity, slipping back yet trying again with those we love, that counters the sadness and leads to hope.

And it's hope that gives us the opportunity to discover the diamonds we have inside us, like the diamond that was missing from Bridget's medal, but through Margaret's gift to Bridget and Bridget's generosity to me, I was able to put the diamond on Ellen's finger.

I don't think of "Margaret's diamond," earned as it was with a spirited, bold, and courageous run in 1951, as a material thing. To me, it's a value, the understanding that life can be full of richness and hope if we give unconditionally and trust in the outcome.

As I walked along the seashore holding Ellen's hand, I realized that learning that principle, that we get when we give, was the gift I had received by saying yes to Bridget and "running" with her.

And so today because of Bridget's generosity, Margaret's diamond sits on Ellen's finger. It connects me to Ellen and others.

It counters sadness and inspires hope.

It gives me love, luck and stability.

It reminds me every day: Step up! Step up!

ABOUT THE AUTHOR

After graduating from the University of Wisconsin, Tom—a life-long runner—first taught in Boston schools where he fell in with the road running crowd. With John J. Kelley, the 1957 Boston Marathon winner, Tom wrote *Just Call Me Jock* in 1982, a history of the Boston Marathon as seen through the eyes of Jock Semple, the colorful race co-director. In 2006, Tom wrote a book about the aviation heroes of 9/11, *Reclaiming the Sky*, which led the president of Fordham University to invite Tom to create an institute—the Human Resiliency Institute—to put healing lessons from the book into programs. The institute's lead program, Edge4Vets, teaches military veterans how to tap their strengths to get jobs. See edge4vets.org. Tom also created a beer called Barb's Beer to raise funds to help cure lung cancer in his late wife (a Boston Marathon runner's) name. Visit barbsbeer.org.

Stay in touch with Tom and learn more about new projects he'll be developing to expand *Runner in Red*, including an essay competition for women to express the joy of running, at runnerinred.com.

MORE ON THE HISTORY OF RUNNING

For those who have had their interest in running and women's running piqued by *Runner in Red*, other books can add to an understanding of the sport, including

Just Call Me Jock: A History and Legacy of Boston's Mr. Marathon, updated version, 2017, by Tom Murphy and John J. Kelley (Barb's Beer Foundation, 2017).

Also consider the following books by these outstanding marathon personalities:

First Ladies of Running: 22 Inspiring Profiles of the Rebels, Rule Breakers and Visionaries Who Changed the Sport Forever by Amby Burfoot (Rodale, 2016)

Boston Marathon: History of the World's Premier Running Event by Tom Derderian (Human Kinetics, 1993)

Marathon Woman: Running the Race to Revolutionize Women's Sports by Katherine Switzer (Da Capo Press, 2017)

Marathon Man: My 26-Mile Journey from Unknown Grad Student to the Top of the Running World by Bill Rodgers and Matthew Shepatin (Thomas Dunne Books, 2013).